WO
TEM

BY
ROBYN DONALD

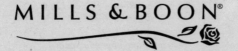

MILLS & BOON®

First published in Great Britain 2002
Harlequin Mills & Boon Limited,
Eton House, 18-24 Paradise Road, Richmond, Surrey TW9 1SR

© *by Robyn Donald 2002*

ISBN 0 263 82924 3

Set in Times Roman 10½ on 12 pt.
01-0402-47228

Printed and bound in Spain
by Litografia Rosés, S.A., Barcelona

CHAPTER ONE

'So THIS is Anne Corbett,' Wolfe Talamantes observed, looking down at the photograph. Damn, he said soundlessly, allowing himself only that small recognition of tension. She was more beautiful than any woman he'd ever met, and that included the film star who'd once shared his bed for some months.

'Rowan Corbett,' the man on the other side of the desk corrected him.

Frowning, Wolfe said bluntly, 'I asked you to investigate Anne Corbett.'

'Her legal name's Rowan Anne Corbett—apparently she was known as Anne until she grew up. She calls herself Rowan Corbett now.'

Carefully monitoring his expression, Wolfe scrutinised Rowan Corbett's countenance, not surprised that she possessed a rare, astonishing beauty. Tony had always had great taste in women—when it came to looks.

Supporting a grave face, her neck rose from a white collar like the stem of a flower. Light summoned a betraying red gleam from the black hair, severely tied back. A soft, stern mouth bloomed against creamy skin. Exotic cheekbones reinforced the sensual promise of that mouth, although the way it was set above a square chin hinted at enough force of character to save her from self-indulgence.

In spite of the guarded wariness in her eyes and the impression of tight, fierce control, for the first time in his life Wolfe understood the potent allure of the forbidden. He found himself thinking of silken skin and a vast bed and fiery, urgent passion.

Grimly he cleared his mind and disciplined his reacting body. He'd expected a temptress, set apart from other beautiful women by exactly that smouldering assurance of carnality.

But those eyes! A smoky meld of gold and topaz and tawny fire, with heavy lids outlined by thick black lashes beneath winged brows. Eyes to turn a man's head, to heat his blood beyond fever and make him forget every other woman. Eyes to drown in, to kill for.

To die for...

Not a fanciful man, Wolfe endured a primeval moment when he thought those eyes had laid claim to him.

Dragging his gaze away from the photograph, he looked at his head of security. 'And she's working in a café in a place called Kura Bay in Northland?'

'Seven in the morning until two in the afternoon, Monday to Saturday.'

Wolfe's brows lifted. If his instinct wasn't playing him false his battle-hardened head of security was as aware of Rowan Corbett's sexual fascination as he was. Reining in an unwanted territorial impulse, he asked casually, 'Liked her, did you?'

The older man eyed him with amusement. 'She seems a nice enough young woman,' he said. 'And looking at her is no problem at all. But she's too young for me, and my wife would cut my throat if I went beyond looking—as you well know.'

Wolfe nodded, accepting the unspoken reassurance. 'Ms Corbett doesn't know that you took this photo?'

'I'm pretty sure she doesn't,' the other man told him.

'But—?'

After a moment the other man admitted, 'She was

pleasant enough, but so distant I did wonder if she was suspicious—until I found out she has a reputation for being aloof.' He added, 'She pots as well.'

Wolfe sent him a disbelieving glance, sharp as an arrow. 'What?'

'Pots. Makes mugs and jugs and bowls from clay on a potter's wheel and—'

'I know how they're made.' Wolfe's tone revealed a rare display of irritation.

His employee smiled. 'They think she's pretty good up there.'

'Any boyfriends?' Wolfe asked in an idle voice at complete variance with his interest in the answer.

'Not a sign of one.' The older man shrugged. 'No girlfriends, either. Keeps herself to herself.'

'Do the locals know about her past?'

'They know, but they won't talk about it. She's the last of an old pioneer family there. Apparently her mother died having her, and her father—a policeman— used to bring her up every holiday to stay with her grandparents, so the locals have known her since she was a kid. These little isolated places are all the same—hotbeds of gossip, but they present a blank face to any outsider. I did learn that she's a martial arts expert.' With a cynical smile, the security expert said on a dismissive note, 'Possibly a handy woman to have around in an emergency.'

'I prefer dirty street-fighting myself,' his boss returned curtly.

His employee, who'd helped him beat off three thugs armed with knives in a stinking South American back alley, grinned. 'That's because you're bloody lethal at it,' he said, reaching for the photograph.

A long-fingered hand flicked it away before he could

touch it. 'I'll keep this,' Wolfe said before he'd had a chance to think.

'OK.' The older man got up. 'Anything else?'

'No. Thank you for that.'

Alone once more, Wolfe unleashed his six-foot four inches from behind the big desk and prowled across to the window. It looked down onto an ordinary street in an ordinary city—a vibrant, noisy mixture of pedestrians, cars and death-defying couriers on their noisy motorbikes. His gaze fell on a group of people dressed in bright Pacific cottons.

Ordinary? No, it could be no other place than Auckland.

Usually it was good to be back in New Zealand, but since the telephone call from his mother he'd felt edgy and aggressive. For six years he'd put Rowan Anne Corbett out of his mind, shutting her away in a box marked, 'Do Not Even Think About Going Here'. But he couldn't ignore his mother.

'Wolfe, I've found the Corbett girl,' she'd said in the quiet, exhausted voice that still made him rage in futile anger.

Within a year of her younger son's death Laura Simpson had succumbed to a condition that robbed her of energy and enthusiasm and the will to live. The best doctors in the world had been unable to give it a name until one bluntly told Wolfe that she was suffering a broken heart.

It was as good a reason as any, Wolfe had thought savagely as he'd demanded, 'How?'

'Just one of those funny coincidences that life seems to specialise in.' She made a soft sound that passed for laughter. 'My friend Moira saw her waitressing in a café in Kura Bay and asked who she was.'

Infuriated by the tremor in her voice, Wolfe asked uncompromisingly, 'Why?'

'Moira was—came to the inquest with me, so she recognised her. She told me when she got back to Auckland, so I wrote to the Corbett girl.' A spark of anger undercut her usual lassitude. 'She did answer—a trite little letter saying that six years ago she'd told the coroner everything she knew about Tony's death. I tried to ring her, but her number's unlisted. I left a message for her at the café, but she hasn't contacted me, so I'm going up to see her next week.'

'You'll do no such thing,' Wolfe said evenly, furious with Rowan Anne Corbett for refusing to satisfy a sick woman's need to talk about her son's wasted death. Even travelling in the helicopter would exhaust his mother. 'I'll see her myself.'

His mother's breath hissed into the receiver. 'Thank you,' she said bleakly. 'And when you do—when you see her—tell her I don't blame her now. I used her as a scapegoat, and I'm sorry about that. She was only twenty-one. But I need to know what really happened that afternoon.'

His mother might have forgiven Rowan Corbett, who had called herself Anne before she became notorious, but Wolfe hadn't. With her red-black hair and her siren's face and body, she'd been directly responsible for his half-brother's miserable death.

Laura hesitated, then asked, 'Wolfe, did you notice any change in Tony after the accident?'

'What sort of change?'

After a short silence she said vaguely, 'I thought he was more serious. More—intense?'

Wolfe frowned. 'I put that down to barely surviving a motorway crash,' he said curtly. 'Experiences like that do tend to make you think more seriously about the important things. It seemed a gratifying step.'

'Yes, of course,' she'd said, and hung up after extracting a promise from him to come to lunch that week.

Now, he looked down at the photograph and smiled, a cold, hard threat that mixed anticipation and aggression. This time Rowan wouldn't get away with lies and subterfuge.

Six years ago a bout of pneumonia had imprisoned him in hospital on the other side of the world, compelling his mother to endure the anguish of his brother's inquest without his support. A man with an ingrained protective instinct where women were concerned, his inability to shield her had cut deep, especially as by the time he got back to New Zealand Rowan Corbett had gone to ground, disappearing without trace.

His protective instincts didn't extend to the woman who'd caused his mother such pain. If he had to force—or seduce—the truth from her, he'd do whatever it took. And enjoy it.

Anne—*Rowan* Corbett had driven Tony to madness, but Wolfe knew he was made of much tougher stuff than his laughing, lightweight, charmingly spoiled brother. Picking up the photograph, he dumped it into his desk drawer and slammed it shut with contemptuous strength.

Half an hour later, his mind haunted by that grave, erotically intriguing face, he swore under his breath and quitted the file he was working on. Without thinking he brought the local newspaper onto his computer screen. And there his eye caught the word, 'Rowan'.

Incredulous, his pulses picking up speed, he leaned forward and clicked on the article, skimming it rapidly before settling down to read it again. A gallery in town was opening a show that night, a mixed collection of

pots and paintings and glassware. According to the re-
viewer, who'd been to a special preview, it was all good
stuff, but he kept his most ecstatic comments for the
potter, whose name was Rowan.

Nothing else—just Rowan.

And the journalist really was ecstatic; phrases like
magnificent glaze, superb form and *inherent plasticity*
jostled off his keyboard. *A brilliant potter,* he trumpeted
at the end; *a shining new star in the constellation of
New Zealand ceramics, and she can only get better.*

Wolfe examined a photograph of one of the bowls.
Elegantly shaped, even on the screen its spare, startling
beauty satisfied some inner yearning for beauty.

He stared at it with narrow, hooded eyes, massaging
the back of his neck with a lean hand. It was too much
of a coincidence—yet Wolfe was a man who often let
hunches tip the balance of a decision. So far, that mysterious instinct hadn't ever let him down. His gut feeling
had taken his stepfather's small electronic firm to international status in the information technology industry.

Formidable intelligence and an uncanny accuracy in
picking trends had also helped that meteoric rise to
power, along with a certain ruthlessness. Yet his adversaries respected him, and his staff stayed with him;
Wolfe expected the utmost from them, but he made sure
they had the best conditions.

He touched a button and said into the communication
system, 'Mrs Forrest, get me a ticket to the exhibition
opening at the Working Life Gallery tonight, please.'

Rowan fought back a nervous attack that came too close
to humiliating panic. 'I don't want to go,' she said thinly,
staring at her reflection in the mirror. An almost total

stranger glowered back at her. Amazing what cosmetics applied by a skilful hand could do!

Bobo Link, her agent, retorted, 'It will do you good! You can't spend the rest of your life hiding.'

Rowan flashed her a glittering glance. 'I'm not hiding.'

'Skulking like a hermit in Northland, slaving your heart out in that depressing little café, refusing to go anywhere and see anyone?' Bobo's voice dripped with sarcasm. 'That's not hiding?'

'I'm busy working! You want pots to sell...'

'So get busy and sell,' said Bobo the ever-practical, who'd tracked Rowan down a year previously and insisted on representing her. Bright, brash, brutally honest, and an agent only because she didn't have a creative bone in her body, she'd become a friend.

Patting Rowan on the shoulder, she went on, 'You look gorgeous—I did a good job with your eyes and mouth even if I say so myself. Fantastic material to work with, of course.'

'You're brilliant,' Rowan told her, relaxing enough to smile. 'I don't recognise myself. But I'm hopeless at selling—that's your strong point! Perhaps I should just stay home and let you do it.'

'Rubbish! People always want to meet the artist, and you're a gift from the heavens because you look so good and photograph so well.'

Rowan said austerely, 'I'm not a pin-up.'

Bobo sighed, but persisted, 'Don't worry, your work stands on its own, but darling old Frank gave you such a brilliant write-up in the paper it would be sinful not to exploit—use it. You're a genius, but you can't eat pots, and if you don't want to go on working in that pathetic café for the rest of your life you'd better turn up at your own first gallery opening.'

'You have such a way with words,' Rowan retorted crisply, examining her reflection more closely. The sheer black and gold silk shirt, courtesy of Bobo, and her own narrow black ankle-length skirt looked good, but her eyes narrowed and she leaned forward. 'All right, I'll come. But I can't wear this shirt—you can see right through it. My *breasts* aren't for sale!'

Rolling her eyes, Bobo said, 'That father of yours has got a lot to answer for. Honestly, you can't—oh, well, yes, if anyone looks really hard they *might* be able to see your nipples through the camisole.'

'A bra?' Rowan said hopefully.

'It would spoil the line. Honestly, Ro, it's almost modest nowadays. *I* wear it like that.'

Rowan grinned. 'You could carry off body paint, but I haven't got the nerve.'

Sighing, Bobo carefully disinterred a black silk garment from her drawer. 'The sacrifices I make! This is brand-new, bought with seduction very definitely in mind, but I'll sacrifice it for you and my ten per cent of everything you sell. No, you won't be able to wear a bra, but you're just big enough to be sexy and small enough to get away without wearing one.'

Rowan eyed it distrustfully. 'What is it?'

'I know you don't live under a tree, so don't pretend you do,' Bobo said grumpily. 'It's a *bustier*, and all it will show is your lovely shoulders.'

'I don't deserve you,' Rowan said simply, and shrugged out of the shirt and into the strapless garment. It clung to her breasts and her slim waist, but at least she was covered. Gratefully she dropped the shirt over her head and looked at herself again.

Bobo snorted. 'You're absolutely right, you don't deserve me, but you look fabulous. Stop whimpering.'

'Whimpering!' Rowan narrowed her eyes and said menacingly, 'Smile when you say that.'

'And that, darling, is your problem,' Bobo told her kindly. 'Your father must have been a wonderful man, but he brought you up to be like the girls *he* grew up with. No, don't fire up—I'm sure he did his best for his motherless daughter, but he was hopelessly old-fashioned. You might *look* sexy and wicked and knowing, but underneath that exotic veneer lurks an innocent Little Red Riding Hood.'

Rowan's mouth dropped. 'Red Riding Hood?' she asked faintly.

Bobo grinned and gave her a hug. 'I know you could dismantle any wolf who came your way, but how on earth would you recognise one?'

How indeed? Rowan thought acidly. She'd taken Tony at face value, and her experience since then hadn't expanded much. Terrified by the havoc emotions could wreak, she'd concentrated on mastering her chosen medium, channelling her strength and intensity into her craft.

'Tonight,' Bobo stated, picking up a bag quilted like a butterfly, 'you're not Rowan Corbett, hermit potter, you're Rowan, a sophisticated, mysterious genius.' Laughing, she added, 'Whose ceramics are soon going to command such huge prices that any sensible collector will buy now while they're affordable. So let's go out and sell!'

Half an hour later, a glass of good New Zealand *méthode traditionelle* sparkling in her hand, Rowan surveyed the room and visualised everyone there in their underwear.

It didn't help. Even when she scattered the underwear with cartoon characters, she couldn't banish the bubble of panic underneath her ribs. She should never have let Bobo persuade her into this. All these people dressed in black, all talking at top speed and all seething with worldliness, totally unnerved her.

She eyed her glass, but decided she'd drunk enough false courage for the moment. Anyway, she was twenty-seven years old; she could handle this. And if she couldn't, it was time she learned to.

'Rowan,' Bobo said from behind, 'here's someone who'd like to meet you!'

A note in her voice warned Rowan that this someone was important and a possible buyer. Bracing herself, she turned.

Beneath Bobo's smile lurked a hint of anxiety. 'Wolfe Talamantes,' she announced. Being Bobo, she automatically fluttered her lashes at the tall man beside her, but his dark green eyes were fixed on Rowan.

Lost in turbulent free-fall, Rowan stared up into a compelling, dangerous face, all hard angles and bold piratical features, while every pulse point in her body thundered with excitement and apprehension. Although the incredibly named Wolfe Talamantes was starkly handsome, his potent magnetism came from within, not from some fortuitous arrangement of genes.

The bubble of panic expanded, but the combination of his name and the memory of Bobo's earlier suggestion that Rowan wouldn't know a wolf if she met one, brought a gurgle of laughter to her lips.

His brows drew together over a nose that would have been straight if he hadn't broken it some time in the past. Instead of coarsening his face, the slight crookedness only added to his dangerous attraction.

'I know,' Wolfe Talamantes agreed drily. A rasp not too far beneath the surface of his voice licked along her nerves like suede across her skin. 'But it's a family name.'

Dry-mouthed, Rowan said carefully, 'I'm sorry, that was rude of me. It's just that my dog is called Lobo.'

Slanted black brows lifted. 'A poodle?' he said with resignation.

She laughed again. 'No,' she said, adding without thinking, 'A truly magnificent German Shepherd.'

In the distance she heard Bobo continue stubbornly, 'Wolfe, this is Rowan. Rowan, Mr Talamantes is interested in Number 47.' She waited, and when neither of them answered finished, 'The green bowl.'

It took all the courage Rowan possessed to force out her hand. 'How do you do?' she said conventionally, her skin tightening as her fingers were swallowed up by lean, cool ones.

'Rowan,' he said in a deep, lazy tone, the line of his mouth curling slightly without softening. Still holding her hand, he said, 'You have great talent.'

To her astonished ears it sounded as though he was making love to her—against his wish, forced to it by a need even greater than his formidable will. Rowan thought she felt lightning flicker around her.

She swallowed and tugged at her hand. 'Thank you,' she said, worried by her brittle words.

This man possessed ten times his share of an intangible male charisma that enveloped her in a dark, swirling charge of energy. Something arrogantly calculated in the way he held that big, powerfully muscled body, a curbed, unreachable assurance, made her both wary and curious, defensive and downright assertive.

A little abruptly, Bobo said, 'Oh, will you excuse me, please? I've just seen someone I really should talk to.'

Wolfe directed a smile towards her. 'We'll be fine,' he said, amusement colouring his sensual voice with its inbuilt note of authority. He looked back at Rowan. 'Won't we?'

Set in lashes sensuously curled at the tips, his eyes were the colour of the darkest greenstone, overlaid by glittering gold specks like gold flakes at the bottom of a deep stream.

Looking into them produced a swift jolt of sensation in Rowan's gut, warning her to listen to her intuition's none-too-subtle command to run from Wolfe Talamantes because he had the power to splinter her world.

'Yes,' she said helplessly. Her breath lodged in her throat as she dragged her attention away from the tough, hard-edged features, trying to remember that she was there to sell her wares. 'Number 47?' she asked in a desperate attempt to sound businesslike. 'Oh, yes, that's a nice piece.' For the life of her she couldn't think of anything more to say about Number 47, except that the glaze was the exact colour of his eyes.

'An extremely nice piece,' he said, his sexily abrasive voice strumming her nerves as his gaze slid over her face to rest for a pulsating moment on her mouth.

Rowan's heart jumped. He was about as subtle as a sledgehammer, but his directness summoned an instant, blatant response from every cell in her body.

Black magic, she thought, turning her head away from those intense eyes and searching for number 47. He had good taste—it was one of her best. Swallowing, she said, 'I had fun with the glaze.'

'You did a brilliant job with it. Where did you learn to pot?'

'Japan.'

Black brows shot up. 'How did that happen?'

Rowan shrugged, trying to ease the tension in her shoulders and neck. 'The potter I admired most in all the world lived in a little village near Nara, so I went to learn from him.'

She felt as though she were in a spotlight, the concentrated focus of his attention burning into her. Her limbs were heavy and slow, her skin tight and unbearably sensitive with awareness, the silk of her shirt and skirt abrading it.

Stop overreacting, she commanded feverishly.

Wolfe said drily, 'Just like that?'

'Well, no,' she admitted with a half smile. 'He didn't want anything to do with me—refused to even see me or the pots I took. I didn't blame him. He was one of Japan's living treasures, whereas I was a total stranger with no credentials—and a woman, a westerner, and only twenty-one.'

'How did you persuade him to take you on?' His tone was neutral, yet something in his voice sent apprehension edging along her spine.

Stiffening it, she told him, 'I camped on his doorstep—at the gate to his garden, actually. Eventually, when he saw I was really serious, he let me show him a pot. He smashed it, but said I could make another, so I did. Which he said wasn't good enough to put in a kiln. After a month of me making pots and him refusing them, he took me on.'

'So he admired your stubbornness.' Wolfe nodded. 'And he recognised your gift, or he'd have let you take root at his gate.'

A hidden warmth took her by surprise. 'He was sheer hell,' she said, her mouth curving in affection. 'He de-

manded the impossible and insisted on complete obedi-
ence.'

'Did you find that difficult?'

His tone set off scrub-fires of sensation through her
body. Searching for something to compare it with, she
decided the closest was the almost physical pleasure clay
gave her when it began to fulfil her vision.

Appalled by the temptation to ignore any meaning in
his words for the sheer, sensuous pleasure of listening
to his voice, she concentrated fiercely and said, 'Very.'

'But you managed to rein in your independence.'

'It was either that or leave. He taught me the way
he'd been taught. The day I refused to do what he
wanted and went ahead on my own, he said I'd learned
all he could teach me and it was time to go. We said
goodbye with the utmost formality, but I wrote to him
every week until he died, and every so often I'd get a
letter back.'

'And how many years were you with him?'

'Five.'

Wolfe Talamantes was standing too close—not that it
would have been too close with any other man, but his
towering presence invaded her boundaries. She took a
sip of her wine and moved a little further away, turning
slightly side on.

'How long do you have to stay here?' Wolfe asked
lazily.

The question startled her. 'What?'

He gave her long, sardonic, dangerously intimate
look. 'How long do you have to stay at this insipid oc-
casion? And don't tell me you're finding it fascinating—
I've been watching you and, although you're hiding it
well, you're bored. Have you had dinner?'

Bristling at the thought of being watched—and worried because he was perceptive enough to see through her social mask—she retorted, 'No, but—'

'Have dinner with me.'

Rowan stared at him, her pulses thudding heavily in her ears. Again every female instinct insisted she refuse and make it stick, yet she knew she was dealing with a pirate—and pirates didn't take no for an answer.

And a more primitive conviction warned her that what seemed like a simple case of sexual interest between one very attractive male and a woman he casually fancied had much darker undertones. In spite of the crackle and hiss of sexually charged air between them, she sensed a deeply buried antagonism.

But perhaps it came from her…

'Stop looking so surprised,' he said, those disturbing eyes gleaming as he surveyed her stunned face. 'You must have had invitations to dinner before. Even in Japan.'

'Not from people I don't know!' she returned smartly.

He grinned, a slightly raffish, nonchalant smile. 'You've been introduced by a friend,' he pointed out. 'That would satisfy the most stringent chaperon—if such a person existed any more.'

She blinked. 'I'm having dinner with Bobo. You could come—' And stopped, flushing, because she'd just about invited him.

'We'll ask her,' he said, and looked across the room. Bobo was chatting animatedly to a man she appeared to know very well, but, as though Wolfe's glance was a laser, she turned. After a quick glance she said something to her companion and began to make her way through the crowd towards them.

When she arrived, Wolfe said smoothly, 'I've just invited Rowan out to dinner, but she says she's booked up with you.'

Bobo smiled sunnily. 'As it happens I've had another invitation too, so it's fine by me. But before you go, Rowan, come across with me and we'll see Georgie.' She smiled at Wolfe Talamantes. 'He's the owner of the gallery, and he wants to talk to Rowan. Do you mind?'

'Of course not,' he said even more smoothly, but as the two women walked across to where Georgie was playing host to an admiring coterie who trusted him to tell them what to think about the various exhibits, Rowan felt the impact of that green gaze squarely between her shoulderblades.

The gallery owner greeted Rowan effusively, announced that more than half her exhibits had sold already, and, after mutual congratulations, presented her to his admirers, who surged about congratulating her.

Expertly extricating her just before her small talk dried up, Bobo urged her towards the private room at the back of the gallery. 'You need info,' she muttered cryptically. Once in the inner sanctum, a cupboard barely big enough to hold them both, she hissed, 'Do you know who Wolfe Talamantes is?'

'No,' Rowan admitted, shocked to find herself worrying that he might be notorious. 'His name sounds familiar—'

'Of course, you don't read newspapers.' Bobo sighed, a frown pleating her brow until she realised it was there and relaxed the muscles.

'I read the headlines in the café newspapers,' Rowan said defensively.

Her agent snorted and leaned closer. 'Not well enough if you don't know him. I'll bet everyone else in New

Zealand does—he's the local boy made good *par excellence*.'

Edgily Rowan said, 'So tell me, who is he? A rock singer? A film star? An All Black?'

CHAPTER TWO

'WOLFE TALAMANTES,' Bobo said deliberately, 'is half-Kiwi, half-Mexican, which explains the name. He's a techno-tycoon and indescribably rich.' She leaned forward for emphasis. '*Hugely* rich, as in billionaire.'

'If he's a techno-tycoon he'll soon be bankrupt, according to the business press,' Rowan shot back, amazed to find herself relieved at that thought. 'See, I do read the newspapers.'

Bobo laughed. 'Not this man. He's no fly-by-nighter—his business is rock-solid. He took over a little electronics firm here in Auckland and turned it into a worldwide affair that's going to take over the universe in five years' time.'

It was in his face, Rowan thought. The arrogant features, straight nose and square chin, the dark, compelling eyes and wide, hard mouth—they all proclaimed the mixture of visionary thinker and ruthless businessman. Aloud she said, 'I didn't realise New Zealand had any really rich people.'

'You'd be surprised.' Bobo nodded knowingly. 'Wolfe Talamantes is a world player, and as tough as they come—well, you only have to look at him to see that, don't you?' She gave a low, throaty laugh. 'He's not married, but of course there have been lovers.'

'And you're throwing me to this wolf?' Rowan asked, her stomach churning with a mixture of alarm and excitement.

Her friend grinned sympathetically. 'I know he's not

the sort of guy to cut your teeth on, but heck, why not give him a whirl? Just remember—it's not likely to be permanent!'

'I dislike promiscuous men,' Rowan said stiffly, 'and I'm only going to have dinner with him, not embark on an affair!' Tony had made no secret of the number of women he'd made love to; he'd seemed to think it would make her even more attracted to him.

Bobo shrugged. 'No sensible person's promiscuous in this day and age. No, he's reported to be a serial monogamist, but ''serial'' is the word to fix on.' She laughed at Rowan's dismayed face. 'Hey, you don't have to go to bed with him if you don't want to, and a couple of dinners will get you some nice publicity, because he's news. I've never heard of him collecting anything except money and beautiful women, but it will be a hugely good thing if he decides to collect pots by Rowan!'

'I don't want that sort of publicity,' Rowan said, angry because she'd been so stupid as to feel a highly suspect, instant rapport with a spoiled tycoon who sounded as though he went through women like a cheese-cutter. And that was underpinned by a foolish jealousy at the thought of those women in Wolfe Talamantes's arms.

'Any publicity is good publicity,' Bobo chanted, adding, 'Don't you dare turn him down now!'

'I didn't really agree to go out with him,' Rowan said, fighting a rearguard action.

'You agreed to dinner—oh, not in so many words, but you made me your excuse for not going, and now that's not a runner. Look,' she said more gently, 'it'll be all right. He might be sex on a stick, but there are no strange stories about him, and there would be if he had any nasty habits. He's a healthy red-blooded male, but, in the words of our great-grandmothers, he's a gentleman. He won't leap on you in the restaurant or drag you off to his lavish apartment and have his wicked way with you. Enjoy a decent dinner with him; that's all you have to do.' She glanced at her watch and yelped. 'Come on, we'd better get out of here.'

The disgustingly rich and successful Wolfe Talamantes stood near the door, and although he didn't appear to be watching for them—being under siege by a glorious redhead in a leather outfit apparently sprayed onto her seductive body—when he saw Rowan come through he said a few words to the redhead, gave her a swift, enigmatic smile that probably sent her blood pressure soaring, and left her pouting but resigned.

The moment his dark eyes fixed on Rowan's and his hard mouth curved into a smile that was a direct challenge, everything but anticipation burned away in a glorious flash of flame, boosting her blood pressure as well.

He said to Bobo, 'Enjoy your evening.'

She coloured a little, but laughed up at him. 'I will. Enjoy yours.'

'Thank you,' he said, but the dark glance that moved to Rowan's face said *I plan to* as he took her arm in a light grip and turned her towards the street door.

Every muscle tensed and fumes of heady awareness filled Rowan's brain, stopping any coherent thought. She had to tell her legs how to move, her body how to walk through the crowd parting in front of them. Under the scrutiny of avid eyes she shivered, yet an aggressive, subversive hunger broke through her defences like upwelling lava—beautiful, dangerous and destructive.

It wasn't solely his chiselled features that attracted attention, nor that disciplined, beautiful mouth, or the loose, relaxed grace of his walk and the startling physical impact of broad shoulders and lean hips and long, heavily muscled legs.

No, the people who tracked their progress across the floor were responding instinctively to the aura of concentrated authority that clung to Wolfe like an invisible cloak, compelling respect.

And his eyes, she thought, watching a girl duck her head and blush when Wolfe looked at her. Enigmatic green with those tiny galaxies of gold imprisoned in their depths, Wolfe's eyes were enough to lose yourself in— eyes that could heat to flames then suddenly chill to the intense colour at the heart of black jade.

'I thought we'd go to Oliver's,' he said coolly as they neared the door.

'Oliver's?' The word sounded clumsy. Embarrassed by the buzz of chatter behind them, Rowan sketched a smile at yet another woman who was watching them with alert, envious interest.

'It's a new restaurant.' He stood back to let her through the door into the foyer.

'We don't hear much about new restaurants in the country,' she commented, striving for lightness as they headed towards the street door.

'Whereabouts in the country do you live?' He opened the outer door, glanced out and went ahead, holding the door for her.

Brushing past him, Rowan wondered why he'd felt it necessary to give that quick, automatic check of the almost empty street.

Duh, stupid, she told herself; even in New Zealand life could be dangerous for men with as much money as Wolfe Talamantes.

The thought of that—and the power his wealth gave him—sharpened her inbuilt caution into edgy wariness.

Wolfe took her arm, ignoring her start of surprise, to guide her to the large car that waited at the kerb.

'I live in Northland,' she answered, deliberately vague.

A man who looked like a retired boxer got out and smiled at them both as he opened the door into the rear of the car. Rowan went in first, sinking into a seat that was infinitely more comfortable than the one in Tony's convertible.

And just remember what too much money did to Tony, she told herself.

Only to have her mind reply wistfully, *But Tony was weak and this man isn't.*

And therefore all the more dangerous. She glanced at Wolfe's square chin and hard profile against the lights outside, looking away while fear kicked in her stomach.

Once he'd clicked his seatbelt home he said, 'Northland covers a lot of ground.'

'It's my home,' she said, forcing herself to speak calmly.

'A woman of mystery,' he said, his tone revealing a smile.

Rowan decided he was probably so confident of his ability to charm that he was sure he'd have her address and phone number by the end of the entrée. She determined not to give it to him no matter how stupidly her wayward body responded to his raw sexuality.

Oliver's turned out to be in a large apartment tower, newly built and oozing the sort of opulence that made her blink.

'The restaurant's more discreet,' Wolfe murmured cynically as Rowan gazed around the massive foyer, a temple to luxury with sofas and flowers and plants against a marble and bronze background. 'It's still going to hurt eyes trained in Japanese restraint, but the food is excellent.'

The waiter had apparently been waiting for them; he smiled as they came in through the door and ushered them to a table separated from the rest of the room by a screen of spiky succulents. Rowan noted a dance floor, small and dimly lit, and a jazz combo playing a sophisticated, eminently danceable tune.

Wolfe ordered French champagne—a famous name she'd read about and never thought she'd taste—and then discussed the menu with her.

Rowan tried to concentrate on choosing, but her eyes kept straying to the dark hands that held his menu, and her ears listened with shuddering pleasure to the sound of his voice.

'So what's it to be?' he asked.

She froze at the impact of compelling green eyes. He knew. He knew just what she was feeling, because he was feeling it too. Intuition warned her that he resented it just as much as she did—and was as helpless to control it.

Her appetite disappearing before a more keen and demanding hunger, she chose the first item her gaze fell upon. 'The mushrooms,' she said, gratified by her steady voice. 'I love mushrooms. And then I'll have fish—the roast salmon. Thank you,' she finished belatedly.

Wolfe ordered soup and steak. A conventional carnivore, she decided, trying to weaken his overwhelming effect by slotting him into a category.

It didn't work.

Neither did consciously relaxing her muscles; as soon as she'd intimidated one set into loosening, the previous ones tightened all over again. Wolfe's primal masculinity challenged everything that was female in her, and she was helpless against it.

Borne reverently by the wine waiter, the champagne arrived, the small ritual of easing off the cork and pouring the golden liquid into two flutes only adding to the fierce intensity flaring between them.

When the waiter had gone Wolfe picked up his glass and said, 'Here's to the future.'

Unease shimmered across Rowan's mind, but she lifted her glass. 'I'll always drink to that. The future.'

Rowan sipped the wine cautiously, then sighed. It tasted like liquid happiness, sparkling with dreams and laughter and sunshine. 'Lovely,' she purred, then added conscientiously, 'I'm sorry I laughed at your name—the connection struck me as funny.'

'At least your own personal wolf is not a lapdog,' he observed drily. 'Where did you get your name?'

'It's a plant name, like Violet and Lily and Rose.'

He nodded, swirling the liquid in his glass with slow, sensuous movements. 'Violets and lilies and roses are flowers, lovely but short-lived. A rowan is something quite different—a tree that's always graceful, with stunning foliage and berries and flowers. Beautiful at all seasons.'

His glance slipped from her face to her breasts, branding them with heat so that they became heavy and alarmingly sensitive against Bobo's *bustier*. Rowan tried to think of that swift survey as a leer, but it was calmly impersonal. His detachment comforted her and disappointed her in equal parts, adding to her confusion.

Sturdily she said, 'My mother fell in love with the berries on her honeymoon, and I was a honeymoon baby.'

Wolfe's smile was as potent as sorcery. 'In parts of

Britain they used to be planted as a protection against witches.'

'There must be lots of witches in this part of New Zealand, then; it's too hot for the trees to grow.'

'So what do you do about witches in Northland?'

Rowan thought she detected something in his words as unsettling as the colour of his eyes.

A moment of cold terror raked her with its claws, vanishing as soon as common sense convinced her that Wolfe Talamantes was not the sort of man to become obsessive. The natural authority that blazed from him was what Tony had envied, and tried to force with his controlling behaviour.

'Witches? Oh, we learn to live with them,' she said, silently applauding the ironic tone she'd achieved. 'Where did your name come from?'

He wasn't surprised at the abrupt change of subject. 'It started off in Germany, but by the time it was handed on to me it had been in my father's family for quite a few generations.' He finished gravely, 'My mother hoped that adding an e on the end might civilise it a little.'

Rowan laughed. 'It's certainly a name that takes some living up to.'

A quick glance at him changed her mind. Although the wolf was a symbol of wildness, of untamed ferocity in a violent countryside, Wolfe Talamantes suited his name in spite of his perfectly tailored clothes and civilised grooming. No one, she knew, achieved success in the cut-throat world of international business without using some particularly uncivilised traits. Like ruthlessness. Her—admittedly limited—experience of rich men was that they used their money as a weapon.

Again that shiver of unease spooked her. She ignored it, because what could he do?

Nothing.

After this dinner she'd say thank you and go back to Bobo's little apartment, and tomorrow she'd return home to Kura Bay and never see him again.

She drank a little more champagne, a small toast to freedom.

'Don't you like the wine?' Wolfe asked. 'I'll order something else—'

'No, it's lovely,' she interrupted. 'Wonderful. Like drinking joy.' She smiled at him, because it wasn't his fault that he reminded her in some ways of Tony.

He smiled back, but she saw a gleam in the greenstone depths of his eyes, and wondered what he was thinking.

'Here comes the food,' she said, hiding her relief as waiters approached the table. 'It smells sublime!'

It tasted sublime too, and as they ate they talked in a civilised manner, discussing books and the theatre and her experiences in Japan. Wolfe had travelled a lot, and enjoyed it; when she asked questions he told her about a recent visit to Khatmandu, and that led to a description of a trip to Mexico at the age of sixteen to see his great-grandfather. He spoke with affection and respect about the country and the effect of another culture on him.

Beneath the dry, almost sardonic sense of humour and the ability to tell a good story Rowan noted a hard, formidable intellect. Not a man to cross—but then she wasn't planning on crossing him. Just keeping out of his way.

'One of these days,' she said, looking with regret at her empty plate, 'I'm going to see the world.'

'You've had the rare experience of living in another culture. Not many of us get to do that.'

She nodded. 'It was a privilege.'

'How long did it take for you to learn to speak Japanese?'

'My mentor didn't speak English at all, so I had to learn in a hurry. I was reasonably fluent in six months. Do you speak Spanish?'

'My father spoke English outside the house, but inside we spoke Spanish, so I grew up bilingual.'

'But your mother came from New Zealand?'

'Yes; she learned Spanish to please my father.' His eyes iced over as if at an unhappy memory, then focused on her. 'When do you go back to Northland?'

'Tomorrow,' she said firmly.

Nodding, he sat back again as the waiter appeared to clear the plates.

Stupidly—tragically—disappointed at Wolfe's calm response, Rowan said brightly, 'I can see why this place is so popular. The food's spectacular, isn't it?'

His eyes mocked her. 'Magnificent.'

The band began to play again, smooth, seductive music that called to her feet.

'Would you like to dance?' Wolfe asked, watching her with half-closed eyes.

'No, thank you,' Rowan said swiftly. Apart from the handshake he hadn't touched her, and that was the way she wanted it.

Well, perhaps not *wanted*, but that was the way it had to be. This strange siren tide running through her body— a sensuous pull that scrambled her brain and melted her bones—was transforming her into a woman so aware of her body and its capacity for pleasure that she almost vibrated with longing.

Dancing was too dangerous to contemplate.

Calling on every ounce of will-power she possessed,

Rowan managed to summon a glossy shield of composure. Occasionally, when the green eyes with their glimmering golden flecks met hers, she lost it, but not for long. Most of the time Wolfe was a perfect host—entertaining, urbane, occasionally caustic, always polite.

And if he noticed those ferociously swirling undercurrents, he ignored them, as she tried to.

Afterwards, in spite of its excellence, she could never remember what the food had been like. She did recall the delicious champagne, and that she'd left the second glass untouched because she needed every brain cell she possessed to carry on this masquerade.

Eventually the meal was finished and she got to her feet. Wolfe came around and took her elbow, his grip burning through the silk of her shirt. Or perhaps it was her skin that was burning.

Between banks of huge lavishly leafed plants they walked past a row of elevators towards the massive foyer, separated from the restaurant by yet more plants and a colonnade. Trying to ignore Wolfe's touch, Rowan made a great play of looking about her.

Across the foyer a woman seated with a group of other people stood up—a tall slim woman of late middle-age, white-haired, with a tired face and an aristocratic profile. Hit by a hammer-blow, Rowan froze, ducking behind a pillar.

Dimly she heard Wolfe's voice, but when the woman began to turn sheer instinct took over. Rowan swivelled and raced back the way they'd come, heart thumping in sick, stupid panic as she tried to get out of there before Tony's mother saw her.

Wolfe's hand on her arm brought her to a sudden halt. Black brows meeting above his nose, he demanded, 'Where are you going?'

'I don't want to be here,' she muttered, white with distress and an odd, furtive terror. 'The restroom…'

No, because Tony's mother could follow her there. She dithered, feeling like a criminal caught in a spotlight.

'The lift,' Wolfe decided calmly, steering her towards the elevators.

Rowan made for the closest, but Wolfe urged her past the lifts and into a small lobby. He took a card from his pocket, thrust it in some sort of lock and another elevator door slid open. From behind them came a burst of chatter in which Rowan was sure she could hear Mrs Simpson's voice.

Desperately she surged into the lift, head turned towards the muted bronze mirror-glass back, waiting for Mrs Simpson to appear and denounce her like the wicked fairy at Sleeping Beauty's christening. Wolfe followed her inside, standing to shield her from the door, and pressed a button.

Instantly and silently the door closed. Slumping, Rowan said weakly, 'Thank you,' as the lift shot smoothly upwards. Shock raced through her in chilling rivulets.

She heard him say something beneath his breath and hard arms enclosed her. It was like being thrust into a furnace, a fiery conflagration she craved with a greed that robbed her of her wits. Rowan dropped her head so that he couldn't read her expression, and if she'd been able to think she'd have wept at her surrender.

'It's all right,' Wolfe said soothingly, his hands splaying across her back.

'I know.' She tried to force herself away from that reviving heat, but her legs refused to support her.

'Just relax,' he said soothingly.

She sagged against him, eyes closed like a coward, lost in a passion so intense she wanted to howl her hunger to the moon. Yet with it came a powerful sense of security that frightened her even more. In Wolfe's arms she felt wildly unsafe—and utterly protected.

He asked, 'What was all that about?' His cool, textured voice insisted on an answer—the voice of the man in charge talking to an underling.

'Just—someone I don't want to meet.' She lifted her weighted eyelids, forcing herself to meet his gaze squarely. 'I'm sorry. It would have been…embarrassing… for everyone. Thanks for saving me from a scene.'

This time she made it out of his arms.

He shrugged, his shoulders in their faultless tailoring wide and somehow ominous against the bronzed mirror glass. 'Like all men,' he said ironically, 'I hate scenes.'

'Like most women too,' she said fervently, and shivered.

'What happened?' Again that cool, impersonal tone, the searching gaze.

Rowan searched for an answer, finally saying weakly, 'It was a misunderstanding.'

'A misunderstanding?' This time his voice expressed polite—and sardonic—disbelief.

She nodded, keeping her eyes lowered. 'Yes.'

Their reflections appeared in the mirrored walls in a dozen different aspects, but all revealed a very tall, very dominant man and a slender woman who barely came up to his shoulder. Feeling miserably vulnerable and fragile, Rowan stared down at the carpeted floor, but before she had time to ask where they were going the lift eased to a halt and the doors slid open to reveal a hall.

'Where's this?' she asked warily, looking around.

'The entrance to my apartment.' He read her expression correctly. Smiling, he went on lightly, 'The least you can do is have some coffee and tell me about this—"misunderstanding". Then I'll take you home.'

'No, no,' she said. 'I'll get a taxi.' But she hesitated.

Another slighter shrug, and an amused drawl. 'Your only alternative is to ride the lifts until he or she goes, and, if he or she lives here, there's always the possibility that he or she will choose the lift you're hiding in.'

'She,' Rowan said numbly, letting him tow her inexorably across to another door. 'It's a she.' She added, 'And I'm not afraid of her.'

He did something to the lock and opened the door. 'Come in,' he said evenly, yet a bite in his words lifted her head.

'I don't think this is a terribly good idea...' she said, dithering again.

Wolfe looked down at her, his mouth a hard, taut line, and for a moment she shivered again. 'I won't jump on you, Rowan.'

'I know,' she said quickly, and foolishly, allowing herself to be persuaded across the threshold.

He smiled before turning to close the door. Almost knocked off her heels by the sheer charisma of that smile, Rowan stared around at a tiled hall, recognising a picture sold at auction a year or so ago for a price large enough to keep her for the next five years.

And worth, she thought after one comprehensive, respectful glance, every cent of that astronomical sum.

As was the Persian rug, an exquisitely sophisticated thing of miraculous colours. So Bobo had been wrong; Wolfe Talamantes was a connoisseur. For some reason this eased Rowan's nerves, but she was still shaking inside when, after another hard glance, Wolfe said, 'Come on, you need that coffee.'

Rowan had never been in a penthouse apartment before. Although she'd expected the same sort of opulence as the foyer downstairs, one glance revealed that Wolfe didn't go in for lavish display. The room he took her into was large, and superbly furnished; it was also comfortable, and not at all ostentatious. Rowan noticed books, more pictures that indicated a collector's eye, and flowers, casually arranged.

'Sit down,' he said. 'I'll make the coffee.'

'Thank you.'

The rush of adrenalin from seeing Tony's mother still surged through Rowan, seeking outlet in action. Waiting until he'd left the room, she wandered across to the long wall of windows and pushed a curtain aside, holding it up as she stared through the glass.

A wide terrace ran outside; her eyes skimmed past furniture to the lights of Auckland, spread around the harbour and reaching out to the blackness of the Hauraki Gulf. Spring rain had washed the air, so that each light twinkled sharp and bright as the Milky Way above her cottage.

More than anything else she longed to be safely back in that cottage with her dog and her own things around her.

'Do you want to go outside?' Wolfe asked from behind her. 'It will be chilly.'

With a curious reluctance she let the curtain fall and turned to face him. 'No, thank you. I was just looking.' She tried a smile, feeling it crack and die. 'You have a glorious view.'

'Come and get this down you.' He put a tray on a low table and straightened as she approached. 'You still look 'pale,' he said, eyeing her keenly. 'This misunderstanding must have been traumatic.'

She shrugged and sat down. 'It happened a long time ago.'

His thick black lashes drooped, hiding his thoughts. 'Really? Judging by your reaction, whatever's going on is very much in the present.'

CHAPTER THREE

WOLFE'S words echoed like a warning in Rowan's super-sensitive ears, although his hard, angular face remained impassive.

'It doesn't matter,' she said dismissively. She'd been so stupid to come here; she had to get out of this place and back to Bobo's.

A muted buzz made her jump. 'What—oh!' as Wolfe reached across and snagged a mobile telephone from the table.

'Sorry,' he said abruptly, after glancing at its tiny screen. 'I have to answer this. Are you all right?'

'Yes, of course.'

When he'd left the room she drank some coffee, grimacing at its strength and the sugar he'd tipped into it. It worked, though; within minutes the subtle stimulation of heat and caffeine and sweetness began to shake off the chill.

Mug in hand, she got to her feet, trying to work off the prowling energy that kept her tense and shivering. The view beckoned again; she looked for some way to pull the drapes back, but couldn't find any cord or rod that might do the trick, so she parted the heavy curtains where they met, holding one up and back so that she could gaze out at the lights.

Tony's mother, she thought, nerves jumping at the memory. What a malevolent trick of fate!

The last time she'd seen Mrs Simpson had been after the inquest. Although the coroner had accepted Rowan's

account of the events leading up to the shot that had
killed Tony and returned a verdict of accidental death,
the older woman hadn't been satisfied. Outside the court-
house, in front of journalists, she had lost control and
accused Rowan of murdering her son, morally if not le-
gally.

Each bitter accusation still echoed in Rowan's ears—
cheat, liar, common little slut.

Appalled and in shock, Rowan had been unable to
defend herself; not that she'd have tried, because behind
the excoriating insults she'd sensed his mother's enormous grief and her bitter inability to accept his death.

Besides, she understood some of Mrs Simpson's loss
of control. Although she knew it was illogical, Rowan
herself blamed Tony for her father's death.

'I'm sorry about that.'

Wolfe's voice, hard and controlled, caught her by surprise. Whirling, she dropped the heavy drape, which hit
the coffee mug, tipping it far enough to fling the rest of
the liquid over Rowan's shoulder and chest.

Stung by the heat, she was unable to prevent a soft
cry of pain and shock.

In a blur of speed Wolfe seized the mug and dropped
it. 'Get your shirt off,' he commanded.

'The curtains—'

'Forget the curtains.' He jerked the silk straight over
her head in one smooth, powerful movement.

'Hey!' she protested, snatching wildly and ineffectu-
ally at Bobo's shirt.

'You're scalded—it has to come off,' he said curtly,
removing the hot, wet *bustier.*

Shocked at the speed of his reactions, and now bare
from the waist up, Rowan shut her eyes and clamped
her arms across her breasts as he scooped her up and

carried her towards the door, one arm around her shoulders, another behind her knees.

'You need cold water on that scald,' Wolfe said shortly, shouldering the door open. 'The kitchen's closest.'

Deep inside Rowan heat flared—taunting, eager, a wildfire response to the flex and torsion of his arms and his body, to his faint, heady male scent as he carried her against his chest through a dining room and into a vast kitchen.

After dumping her on her feet in front of the sink, he grabbed a teatowel from a drawer and ran it under the tap. 'Hold it against your skin,' he ordered.

Rowan pressed the cloth over her skin, welcoming the soothing coldness with an involuntary sigh and the covering with relief.

'Thank you,' she said in a ragged voice. 'I hope the clothes are all right—they belong to Bobo.'

'If they aren't I'll replace them,' Wolfe told her, holding another cloth under the tap.

'And the curtains and the carpet—'

'To hell with the curtains and the carpet,' he said with suppressed violence. 'They'll clean.'

Startled, Rowan looked up into eyes as glittering and green as a predator's. Her mouth dried, but she said sturdily, 'There's coffee all over them. I'll pay—'

'How does your shoulder feel?'

'It's stinging a bit, but it's all right.'

'Do you need a doctor?'

'No,' she yelped. 'It's barely a scald—see?' She lifted a corner of the teatowel. The flush was fading from her skin as fast as the smarting.

'It's fine,' she said, uncertainly this time, hardly able

to articulate because a primitive hunger stripped away everything but a stark, forbidden need.

Remember, Tony was rich and charismatic too, she warned herself, striving to kill the desire. But Tony had been cunning and obsessive, determined to take by force what she wouldn't freely give him.

So how do you know Wolfe isn't the same?

Turning away from him as she clamped the wet tea-towel back onto the skin, she listened to an obstinate intuition reassure her that Wolfe showed nothing of the manipulative greed for possession that had driven Tony.

She certainly hadn't felt anything like this potent fascination for the other man. Gratified at first because of Tony's open admiration, it hadn't taken her long to realise that her liking went no deeper than the surface, whereas one look from Wolfe's green eyes had summoned her from a long sleep, waking her to life and colour and a perilous, fascinating invitation to feel again.

Wolfe felt it too—she read it in the line of colour along his high cheekbones, in the molten intensity of his eyes as the air turned to fire between them.

'Let me see,' he said, waiting as she revealed the skin again.

Her heart shook as he touched her shoulder, a gentle pressure with the back of his hand that sizzled through her like lightning, blocking the breath in her lungs.

And then he stepped back. 'Your skin's still hot. As soon as that cloth stops feeling cold, change it to this one,' he said curtly, dropping the second wet teatowel onto the granite bench.

Horrified by her wild response, Rowan watched him walk out of the kitchen. Hastily she changed the cloths, holding the discarded one against her hot cheeks as she ached for something she could never have.

She didn't hear him come back into the room, so she jumped at his mocking voice—and the raw undernote he couldn't conceal. Nor could he conceal the stripped, stark angles of his face, or the predatory gleam in his eyes.

'Hiding, Rowan?'

If she gave him one signal he'd take her to bed. And she'd go with him, eagerly.

She lowered the cloth from her face. 'No,' she said defensively.

He showed her a tube of green gel. 'Aloe vera, which is exceptionally good for minor burns. Do you want to put it on in the bathroom?'

'Yes, please. And Bobo's shirt.' Colour burned along her cheekbones, but she continued sturdily, 'I'll collect it on the way.'

'I've dumped it in a tub of cold water. I'll bring you one of my shirts.'

Rowan did not want to wear Wolfe's shirt—it was altogether too intimate—but her skin crawled at the prospect of huddling back into wet clothes for the ride home. 'Thank you,' she said in a muted voice.

The bathroom he took her to was big and sparely luxurious with marble and glass and heated towel rails and vast mirrors.

Gazing at a set of plumbing that looked as though it needed an engineering degree to make it work, Rowan tried to lighten the crackling tension by asking in a disappointed voice, 'No gold taps?'

With a glinting, sardonic glance he returned, 'Sorry.'

Unlike Tony, he wasn't a man who needed the quick ego trip of expensive accessories. Everything in this palatial penthouse was something he liked, and that was why the place looked so good; it was an expression of his personality.

Her bowl would fit in here…

Wolfe put out a long-fingered hand and dropped the tube of gel onto the marble vanity. She didn't want to look up, but compelled by an urge she understood too well, she flicked a swift glance into the mirror.

Only to have it snared by his eyes. He loomed over her like some Dark Lord of Hades, she thought, catching her bottom lip in her teeth for a second before wrenching her gaze away.

'I'll get you that shirt,' he said, tension rasping through the words.

She waited until the door closed silently behind him and let her breath out in a quiet hiss. Slowly, reluctantly, she lowered the cloth and stared at her body in the mirror. The scald had faded to soft pink; beneath it her breasts still throbbed, their peaks tightly budded in a primal response to the turmoil in her body. Had Wolfe liked what he'd seen?

Oh, yes, she thought grimly, uncapping the tube. He'd liked it. But then most men responded easily to smooth female skin and soft breasts. Beneath her fingers the gel sank in, easing the last of the pain away.

She was screwing the cap back on when she heard him knock at the door. Snatching up the nearest towel, she held it across her breasts and called, 'Come in.'

He opened the door and tossed in a white T-shirt. 'Try that,' he said, and disappeared, closing the door firmly behind him.

The perfect gentleman, even if he had ripped her clothes from her. A hot little shudder worked its way down her spine, turning her bones to rubber. She squirmed at the hard tug of desire in the pit of her stomach.

Repressing it, she got into the T-shirt, smiling as she bunched it around her. He was even bigger than she'd thought; his smooth-knit co-ordination and grace hid his size.

At least this huge T-shirt swathed around her would stop any hint of seduction in its tracks! Yet she felt oddly vulnerable as she emerged and found her way back to the sitting room.

He'd cleaned up the spilt coffee, although her gaze flew guiltily to the dark marks on the curtains and the carpet.

'It doesn't matter,' he said briefly, getting up from a chair as she hovered in the doorway. 'I've poured you another cup.'

'Thank you.' She made her way across the room and collapsed into the sofa. The T-shirt billowed around her before settling. 'And thank you for the loan of the shirt,' she said as she picked up her coffee.

'How's your shoulder?'

'It's fine. It was hardly a scald, and the aloe vera has taken away the sting. It's wonderful stuff, isn't it? I have it growing in my garden.' Rowan knew she was chattering inanely, but she needed to throw up barriers.

The balance had altered. Wolfe had seen her breasts, touched her skin, and she was wrapped in his shirt; intimacy hung like a heavy perfume in the tense air, mindless and erotic, smoking through her body and her brain.

Mrs Simpson or not, she had to get out of here!

Taking temporary refuge behind the coffee, she drank some gratefully before setting the mug down sharply. 'Could you call a taxi, please?'

'I'll take you home,' he said abruptly.

'A taxi will be—'

'Rowan.' His voice was cool and silky, a warning in itself. 'I'll take you home. Finish your coffee.'

'Has anyone ever told you,' she asked with spurious brightness, 'that your sort of man—the high-handed, masterful type—went out of fashion thirty years ago?'

'Plenty.' He got to his feet and crossed the distance between them in two long strides. 'Has anyone ever told *you* that you're bloody dangerous?'

Her mouth dropped slightly open, but before she could think of a brisk reply to fling back he added, 'As in dangerously desirable…'

The words hung in the air as he drew Rowan to her feet. It was no swift, brutal clutch, and she might have been able to resist him if he hadn't spoken, hadn't looked at her with such open, untamed hunger.

This, she thought with something that felt like relief, had been inevitable from the moment they'd set eyes on each other. Tomorrow she might regret it, feel shame, but now, with that passionate seeking coiling through her, she knew it was the only right way for the evening to end.

'I want to kiss you,' he said between his teeth, hands tightening on her shoulders.

One kiss wouldn't shatter her soul. She didn't move. 'And I want to kiss you.' Was that her voice, low and husky?

Deliberately, her pulses pounding, her limbs heavy with the same languor that weighted her lashes, she put her hand over his heart. As it jumped beneath her palm, lean fingers closed around hers, tanned skin overwhelming pale.

Ignoring the warnings that clanged in her mind, she

breathed his name—'Wolfe'—as though she'd been waiting down the ages for it, and smiled.

Instead of the kiss she'd expected, he looked long and deep into her eyes—claiming her, she thought dazedly, in a wordless, primitive takeover, a conqueror asserting his power, making her his for ever. Yet even that wasn't enough to stifle her senses, now thrumming with erotic input.

When his gaze had stripped away her defences, he bent his head and claimed her mouth too, wiping everything from her mind but her need to follow where he led.

Dimly she thought, *I don't even know this man*, and her heart said, *So?*

She suspected she had always known he existed, unconsciously yearned for him and needed him, so this joining was the culmination of aeons of frustrated desire. More than anything in this world she wanted him—more than peace of mind, more than love, more than life itself.

'Are you sure?' he asked, but his eyes, his voice, his knowledgeable hands revealed his confidence.

Her gaze still imprisoned by the blazing greenstone of his, she caught his free hand and held the palm against her cheek, before turning her face into the strong warmth of it and kissing the palm. 'More than sure,' she told him. 'Show me.'

Narrowed eyes scorched across her skin and came to rest for vibrant, humming moments on her mouth. 'Show you what?'

'Everything.'

His smile was crooked, without humour. 'Dangerous indeed,' he said. 'So be it.' The harsh words had the inexorable ring of an incantation.

And he kissed her again. Lost in passion, she yielded,

just as desperate, just as starving, just as eager for ful-
filment as he was, drowning in the heat of his mouth
and her own incandescent responses.

'You are so beautiful,' he said against her throat. 'I
want to touch you, see you, take you.'

'Yes.' Although she whispered the word soundlessly,
he heard it.

Slowly, so slowly that every cell in her body
thrummed with expectation, he eased his big white T-
shirt to one side so that he could kiss the place where
her neck joined her shoulder.

At least she thought he was going to kiss it; when he
nipped her there she shuddered at the exquisite sorcery
of the exotic little caress.

On the rare occasions when she'd speculated about
making love she'd always imagined that removing
clothes had to be awkward and embarrassing, but Wolfe
made it a seduction in itself; unhurriedly, his expression
absorbed and serious, he eased the shirt over her head,
kissing the pale skin his leisurely skill revealed until at
last he looked down at the soft flushed skin of her
breasts.

Tormented by the need for some unknown caress, they
ached. Rowan felt the nipples bead into little nubs as
sensation abraded them, a sensation that flamed to amal-
gamate with the fire building rapidly in the pit of her
stomach.

All she could see in Wolfe's dark face was that complete concentration, tanned skin tightening over his
proud bone structure so that he looked like some mythic
warrior.

When he lifted his eyes she gasped at the naked heat
and desire she saw in their depths. A barely articulated
noise in his throat echoed through her. She drew back

fractionally, but he reached for her and crushed her mouth beneath his, and this time he didn't stop when he broke the kiss but travelled further, until his seeking mouth found one of the aching peaks.

Rowan cried out, her fists clenching in his hair, holding the sweet, sharp torture closer. He suckled, gently at first and then more strongly as shivers racked her, turning her bones to jelly, sending messages of need and fierce surrender through every cell, messages that coalesced with white-hot speed at the centre of her desire.

Just how she got to the sofa she never remembered, but even as she registered the cushions across her back her skirt was being stripped from her, and with it her briefs.

For years Rowan had believed that Tony's stalking had frozen her ability to feel desire, but occasionally in that semi-conscious state between sleep and wakefulness she'd imagined making love to an unknown lover. Always in her dreams she'd been shy, embarrassed by the raw power of the process, unable to visualise what the faceless lover would do.

One glance at Wolfe had smashed through the shield she'd erected around herself, and now his hard-edged, autocratic face would be forever stamped on her fantasies, his disciplined grace would prowl for ever through her dreams.

She watched from beneath her lashes as he unbuttoned his shirt, lean brown hands working deftly. Slowly her gaze wandered across the tanned, sculptured torso, thrilling to the contrast between sleek tanned skin and the patterned whorls of fine hair.

Muscles flexing and bunching, he shrugged free of his shirt and dropped it. Like something out of a dream world, a place where the archetypes held true and heroes hunted dragons through the mountains, he looked down at her, sleek and magnificent and potent as some great beast of prey.

His hands dropped to his belt; he began to unbuckle it. Dry-mouthed, Rowan stared into the face of a conqueror—and caught a glimpse of her own unsuspected power, her own strength. Her wondering eyes snared by his, she lost herself in the golden, glinting galaxies that smouldered like stars in explosion.

Fool's gold, she thought as her lashes drifted down, but the words echoed emptily, without resonance. She was stripped of any awareness except of the sensations rocketing through her.

Powerful and menacing as a thundercloud, yet pierced by light, Wolfe's maleness demanded all that was female in her.

The sofa gave as he came down beside her. Lightning arced from his fingertip when he traced the shape of her lips, the high sweep of her cheekbones, the arch of her brows, and her lashes. 'Look at me,' he murmured huskily.

'I burn up when I do,' she mumbled.

He laughed beneath his breath. 'And you think I don't? Touching you is like riding the storm. Look at me.'

Obeying, she recognised the feral heat of passion in his skin, the glitter of it beneath his eyelids, its force in the mirthless smile curving his mouth.

'Now touch me,' he said quietly.

The hot, silken texture of his skin was only slightly roughened by the hair that proclaimed his masculinity. Rewarded by the rapid drumbeat of his heartbeat, Rowan moved her hand tentatively to follow the contour of a muscled shoulder. It tensed beneath her touch, and her eyes flew upwards.

'Did you think you were the only one affected?' he asked, the words edged with a spice of mockery. 'We're in this together, Rowan.'

But for him this was not new and unexpected.

He must have seen the shadow in her eyes because he leaned down and kissed her mouth.

'Together,' he said again, and it was all the reassurance she needed.

Her fingers ventured further, found a small crescent scar on his back and committed it to tactile memory. Smiling, she adjusted her body against the iron-hard length of his; heart singing with frantic excitement, she let him lead her where he wanted to go.

With ardent mouth and clever hands and experienced, arousing earthiness, Wolfe guided her to realms of sensuality Rowan had never imagined. She was filled with the taste of him and the scent of him and the feel of him. And he was gentle—as though he knew that for her this was the first time.

Perhaps he did. Slowly, skilfully, he built the fire inside her with the heat of his mouth on her skin, introducing her to sensations so glittering and exotic that she lost any anchorage in time and space, her whole world contracting to the man who made love like a dark angel.

When at last he moved over her she was glowing and eager, all forebodings wiped away by his clever hands and passionate expertise. The muscles along his jaw and in his arms and shoulders bunched as he fought for control, but slowly, carefully, he eased himself over her. 'Rowan?' he asked harshly.

Opening her dazzled eyes, she fixed them on his. Her body clamoured for something she didn't yet recognise, something she had never known, yet craved. It was too late for tenderness; untamed, ferocious hunger overpowered her. She slid her arms down his back, feeling the iron restraint he'd imposed on himself—imposed on her—and she couldn't bear it. Her hands clung to his narrow hips; surrendering to her feverish hunger, she arched, enfolding him, making him hers.

He thrust into her in another primitive, desperate claim, burying himself so deep that the shock wave of his possession reverberated through her, the stab of pain passing almost unnoticed.

I'll never be the same again, she thought dizzily, already wanting more.

Overwhelmed, she whimpered, and he kissed her, letting her get accustomed to the uncompromising male invasion until the feeling of fullness, of unbearable stretching, eased, and her hips tightened against him with involuntary insistence.

Wolfe began to move and she moved with him, awkwardly at first and then with confidence, with pleasure, with languorous hunger. Sensation gathered, spiralled through her body in concentric rings; soon she was aware of nothing but Wolfe's driving mastery of her responses and the heightening need to strive for some pinnacle, some unknown goal...

And then she reached it in a searing conflagration of unutterable excitement and release, of explosive, rapturous power.

He seemed to contain the force of her orgasm and feed on it, yet somehow channel it back to her, strengthened and intensified so that she was flung by the waves of violent ecstasy into yet another dimension. Simultaneously she shuddered at the raw, masculine force of his release—a sense of taking and being taken, of meeting and matching, of complete union.

When it was over, when the last delicious sensation had died away to utter satiation, Rowan began to shiver. Their wild mating had taken something from her; she felt as though half her soul had been riven away.

'Don't cry,' Wolfe murmured. 'It's called the little death, but it's not the end of the world...'

Frowning, he got to his feet and looked down at her, then picked her up and carried her through the apartment and into a large bedroom.

'I don't know why I'm doing this,' she wept, keeping her eyes closed against the light. 'I never cry.'

'It will wait until morning,' he told her in a sombre voice, bending to pull back the covers on an enormous bed and slide her between them.

For a moment she thought he was going to leave her, but although he paused it was only for a moment before he joined her.

'Go to sleep,' he said, the abrasive texture of his voice very pronounced, and pulled her against him.

She should go back to Bobo's, she thought, but his warmth tempted her so that she went gratefully, lying half across him, her head tucked into his shoulder. His arm was warm and heavy around her, promising protection and support in an offer she couldn't accept.

Soon she'd get up and leave him...

Soon she'd suffer the fate of all who taste forbidden fruit—exile into a bitter kingdom of emptiness where nothing would ever be the same again. But not just yet.

He smoothed back a lock of hair from her face. 'It was the first time for you?'

Very slightly she nodded.

'Did I hurt you?' he asked.

'No.'

Silence, during which her tears dwindled and evaporated and the racing of his heart beneath her ear declined to an even, solid rhythm.

Outside it had begun to rain; she could hear the drops hissing against the window.

Dreamily she said, 'I didn't know it would be like that.'

'It usually isn't.' His voice hardened. 'You're the first virgin I've made love to, but it's not usually as…'

'Earth-shattering?' she supplied when he paused.

His chest lifted; surprised, she looked up and realised he was laughing silently, his half-closed eyes green with mockery. And something else, something she recognised as bleak acceptance.

'Rowan,' he said. 'Rowan Corbett. Did you know that Corbett means raven?'

'Yes. Why?'

'It's an omened bird. It does seem appropriate with that black hair.' He pulled a strand down and curled it around her breast. The light, soft touches of his fingers on her sensitised skin trailed fire.

Coolly, deliberately he said, 'You have an elemental power.' His tone was distant, almost impersonal, yet a molten note ran beneath the unhurried words, and there was nothing detached about the way he was caressing her. 'When I look at you I see the pagan goddesses of Minoa with their bare breasts and ringlets and flounced skirts presiding in some ancient rite over an adoring, awe-struck congregation.'

'I'm perfectly ordinary,' she said, stumbling over the words and closing her eyes against the oddly stirring juxtaposition of his tanned hand playing with her black hair against the creamy pallor of her breasts.

'I don't think so,' he said in an abstracted tone, 'and I don't think you believe that either.'

Silken curls whispered over her skin, setting her tingling. Languorous heat spread from the pit of her stomach, following secret paths as he arranged her hair across her breast and his chest. Then he bent his head and kissed her breast through the sable mass.

'No, not yet. You need time to recover,' he said, when eventually her wordless murmur and the slow, erotic movements of hips and legs signified her surrender.

Instead he showed her other ways in which she could be pleasured, until she cried out and sobbed, and again rode the whirlwind of her release.

It was exquisite, but it was not the same. The ferocious intensity, the driven desire was no longer present. Perhaps he too needed to reach a climax for her to feel it.

She said, 'What about you?' and then blushed for the crassness of her words.

'Don't worry about me,' he said. 'Go to sleep now.'

And such was the magic of his deep voice that she slid into an unconsciousness free of any dreams.

Frowning, Wolfe looked down at her beautiful face with night-accustomed eyes, a swift kick of desire hardening his big body when his gaze roved the sensuous mouth, still slightly swollen from his kisses. Why had she let him make love to her? Had seeing his mother in the foyer tipped her so far off balance she'd sought comfort wherever she could?

It didn't seem likely for such a determined virgin, yet in his arms she'd loved him with a heart-shattering combination of earthy sensuality and innocence that had temporarily banished everything but the need to possess her.

She didn't know who he was. And, thank God, his

mother hadn't seen her. Her call to ask him to lunch the following day had stiffened his resolution to do whatever was needed to find out what had happened to his half-brother.

Why the hell hadn't Rowan made love with Tony?

The answer slid like a stiletto into his mind. To keep him dangling, of course. Until Rowan, Tony had probably never had a woman refuse him; one who did would have his appetite with the powerful charm of novelty, of challenge.

Innocent or not, she was a worthy opponent, he thought grimly. She'd read Tony like a book, and she'd made a pretty good stab at understanding Tony's brother too, probably guessing that he'd find coyness and virginal qualms irritating.

Wolfe listened to the soft sigh of her breathing, berating himself for not using the time better. He might have been able to coax the truth from her after they'd made love. He hadn't even thought of it. Angered by his weakness, he eased her back onto her pillow, hardening his heart when she made a soft noise of protest and turned to him.

He needed space. And he needed to think with his usual clarity, not with a brain clouded by the fumes of sex and an unappeased, gripping hunger that still prowled through his body.

So what did she plan next? An affair involving the skilful transfer of a considerable sum of money from his pocket to hers?

Wolfe gave a slow, tigerish smile as his body tightened. He'd have considerable—and dangerous—pleasure seeing that she earned it.

The smile vanished in a flash of chagrin. Of course it was impossible, even though it was probably the easiest way of finding out exactly what had happened six years previously, when Tony had gone to her father's house to ask for her hand in marriage and died there, shot through the heart by her father's target pistol.

He could still woo her, win her confidence, and eventually persuade her into telling him the truth.

Yet there was always the possibility that she knew he was Tony's half-brother, that her reaction to his mother's presence in the foyer tonight had been more calculated than involuntary.

Perhaps she hoped to dazzle him into calling his mother off? It would certainly explain her capitulation, her enthusiastic, heart-shaking passion. If so, she'd learn that he wasn't as easily manipulated as his brother.

CHAPTER FOUR

ROWAN woke to a gentle rise and fall beneath her cheek, to heat, to the regular sound of someone breathing. To darkness.

Freezing, she searched through the tumbled fragments of thought in her brain, struggling to recall where she was, and what—

Wolfe. *Wolfe Talamantes.*

The full enormity of what she'd done hit her with enough impact to stop her heart. Last night, freely and without shame, she'd made love to a man she'd only met a few hours before—a man even richer and infinitely more charismatic than Tony.

At least he'd used protection, she thought grimly, listening to the steady beat of his heart against her cheek.

One glass of champagne was no excuse. Neither was the shock of seeing Mrs Simpson in the foyer. The truth was she'd wanted Wolfe from the moment she'd met his warlock's eyes, and because it had been an evening out of time, out of her life, she'd snatched the opportunity when it arose.

But that was last night, and although she felt warm and oddly secure in his bed, right now she had to get the hell out of there; staying would be courting heartbreak.

It would be very easy to fall fathoms deep in love with Wolfe Talamantes, and she had only to remember Bobo's hissed information about him to know that they had nothing in common beyond an instant and apparently mindless lust. Apart from the terrifying amount of money and power he controlled, he wouldn't marry a woman who was never so happy as when she was elbow-deep in clay.

And she didn't want an affair; with bitter irony, she realised that she could become very possessive of Wolfe. No, not as possessive as Tony had been, but enough to humiliate.

Time to get out, she told herself, bracing for a swift, noiseless departure.

Wolfe woke—silently and smoothly—before she had time to do more than react with a jolt of stupid panic. She thought fuzzily that she could even discern the moment that swift brain realised she was there. He knew she was awake too, because he said her name.

'Yes,' she answered thinly, pulling herself free of his arms to scramble across to her side of the bed, cringing at her nakedness.

'What are you doing?' he demanded in a rasping, sexy voice.

'I'm going,' she said stonily. But her calm deserted her when he began to move. 'No—no, you don't need to get up,' she gabbled. 'I'll get dressed—' She groped around for her clothes, remembering too late that they were still in the sitting room. Desperately she finished, 'And then I'll ring a taxi.'

But she couldn't move, because she was going to have to walk nude out of the room. Why worry? some sadistic part of her brain taunted. He's seen and touched and kissed every inch of your skin...

At least he didn't turn on the light.

He didn't try to persuade her to stay, either. 'I'll take you home,' he said evenly.

'You don't have to—'

'I'll take you home,' he repeated, flinging back the bedclothes.

Rowan fled.

By the time Wolfe appeared in the sitting room she had pulled on her clothes, including his T-shirt, and was looking despairingly for her evening bag with its comb.

'On the floor beside the sofa,' he told her curtly.

She pounced on it and turned her back as she opened it. Her skin told her when Wolfe left the room. Wincing, but ruthless, she dragged the comb through her tangled hair, wrenching out the last knot when he returned, this time carrying a plastic bag.

'The wet clothes,' he said neutrally.

Yet she knew he was furious—not with a swift flash-fire that would soon be over, but with a deep, burning anger.

With as much formality as she could produce, she said, 'Thank you.'

In a way his lack of response made it easier. Silently they rode down the lift into the basement car park, silently they got into his car, and after she'd given him Bobo's address they drove without speaking through streets wet with spring rain, Rowan clutching the plastic bag tensely.

'Do you have a key?' he asked as the big car drew up quietly outside the block of apartments.

'Yes, thank you.'

'We need to talk,' he said abruptly. 'I'll call around tomorrow afternoon.'

'I—there's no need to—'

'Rowan, either we talk tomorrow or I take you back home and we talk now,' he said, his pleasant tone not hiding the threat behind the words.

'I'm not going back with you now,' she flashed. 'All right, I'll be here tomorrow.'

He came with her up to the door, said a courteous goodnight, and left once she'd let herself inside.

That was when her heart began to beat again, her breath to fill her lungs. Suddenly weak, she sagged against the wall a moment before stiffening her spine and tiptoeing through the apartment.

In the tiny second room that doubled as guest room and Bobo's office, she lay in the bed and stared at the ceiling until night paled into dawn.

Why had he been so angry? Because he'd lost some part of that formidable control when they made love?

Because they'd made love? That she could under- stand. It had been crazy—so out of character for her she couldn't believe she'd behaved with such abandon. Although it had been the most transcendental experience of her life, she'd expected her first experience to be with someone she trusted, not someone she'd fallen instantly in lust with—a man she didn't even know.

And she suspected that Wolfe didn't normally lose it as completely as he had last night. Thoughts buzzing fruitlessly around her tired brain, she eventually slipped into a troubled sleep.

'All right,' Bobo said, whirling around as Rowan walked into the kitchen the next morning, 'tell me—' She broke into a little crow of laughter. 'No, you don't need to tell me—I can see what kept you out until three o'clock. Is he as good as the rumours say he is?'

Rowan managed a weak smile. 'I don't kiss and tell.'

'Sit down, sit down—you need some caffeine.' Bobo poured coffee and brought it across, her eyes snapping with interest. 'What's the matter?' she asked. 'And don't tell me he's lousy, because I won't believe it. No one could give off sparks like Wolfe Talamantes and be a loser in bed.'

Rowan drank some of the coffee and managed to summon a smile. 'All right, I won't tell you,' she said.

Bobo frowned, easing herself into the other chair at the tiny table. 'Feeling bad?' she asked with concern.

After gulping more coffee, Rowan gave in to the temptation to confide. 'I was stupid. I mean—making love with someone I'd never seen before! Crazy.'

'Why? If you both enjoyed it, what's the problem?' Bobo sounded honestly bewildered. 'You did make sure he used protection?'

Rowan flushed, but said, 'I wasn't that far gone.'

Nodding, her much more sophisticated mentor said, 'Good. So I suppose this morning-after angst is a hangover from your strait-laced dad. OK, listen to big sister, here—it's time you grew up and joined the twenty-first century. Trust me, it's no big deal. You've got to kiss a lot of frogs, et cetera, and some of them you're going to enjoy kissing. I'd really enjoy kissing Wolfe Talamantes myself, no matter where it was going, but one look at you and he didn't even see me.' She said it without rancour. 'Don't go all prissy on him now.'

'I doubt if I'll see him again after today,' Rowan said wearily.

Bobo gave her a shrewd glance. 'He wants to see you again?'

'He's probably going to apologise,' Rowan told her with gloomy foreboding. 'He said we had to talk.'

More than anything she wanted reassurance, but Bobo frowned. 'Doesn't sound good, but, hey, if it was a classic one-night stand he wouldn't even be thinking about contacting you again. He must be interested.'

'Even if he is, it won't work.'

Bobo's brows shot up so high they were lost in her hairline. 'Why not?'

Rowan gave an incredulous laugh. 'I can't see myself as a billionaire's girlfriend, can you?'

'Stop that right now! I can see you as anything you want to be,' Bobo said trenchantly. 'Rowan, don't go running back to Kura Bay; at least give him a chance! It will do wonders for—' She stopped, looking self-conscious.

Rowan forced a dry smile. 'Not even for your ten per cent am I going to do something that's not right for me.' She stared down into the dark depths of her mug. 'And this is not right for me,' she said heavily. 'It's so wrong it scares me. He's everything I swore I'd never get tangled up with again. And he's far too attractive.'

Bobo sighed. 'I suppose you've fallen for him. OK, it happens. The thing to do is pick yourself up and find another one. There are lots of men out there, and a lot of them are good ones. Did your father try to convince you that everybody has a soulmate, and that you should wait for him?'

Rowan recalled the man who'd never looked at another woman after his bride of less than a year had died giving birth. 'No,' she said quietly.

'But that's what you'd like,' Bobo said, nodding. 'It's what we'd all like, but it's not going to happen, Rowan. People who search for soulmates are true romantics— and you won't find Wolfe Talamantes in that rank. He's far too tough to believe in pretty fairytales. Besides, what happened to his brother would have put him off the soulmate thing for life.' At Rowan's enquiring look she shrugged. 'Oh, it's an old scandal. He shot himself because he couldn't get the girl he wanted. She wasn't willing, apparently. Rowan—Rowan, what's the *matter*?!'

White-lipped, Rowan asked, 'What was his name?' When Bobo just stared at her she demanded harshly, 'Wolfe's brother—do you know his name?'

'I don't—yes, yes, I do. He was his half-brother— Tony Someone—I remember because I was going out with Tony Weatherly then.'

'Tony Simpson.' Rowan dropped her face in her hands. 'Oh, God,' she whispered, icy with shock and dismay.

Bobo swallowed. 'You,' she whispered. 'Were you the girl? No, I'd have remembered your name.'

'Rowan is my first name,' she said thinly, 'but my father always called me by my second name, Anne. I don't think he could bear to call me Rowan because my mother chose it before I was born. I decided to call myself Rowan after the—afterwards.'

Stunned, Bobo got up and hugged her fiercely. 'Oh, what an awful coincidence! And neither you nor Wolfe knew!'

Sheer horror froze the blood in Rowan's veins. Had he guessed? She tried to recall the moment she'd seen Mrs Simpson in the foyer—where had Wolfe been? Behind her, and to one side, shielded from the seated group by a screen of plants and one of the huge marble pillars. And once Rowan had blundered towards the restaurant he hadn't looked back—his whole attention had been on her.

No, he couldn't have seen or heard his mother.

He certainly wouldn't have made love to Rowan if he'd known who she was. Flooded with ridiculous relief, she said thinly, 'Neither of us.'

Bobo stepped back, eyeing her with concern. 'Are you going to tell him?'

She couldn't. 'His mother blames me for Tony's death, so I presume Wolfe does too.' Painfully relinquishing barely formed dreams and hopes, she said, 'Bobo, I have to go home. Right now. But if I do, he'll want to know where I am.' Of course, he might be relieved.

Bobo was obviously dying to probe further, but something in Rowan's face stopped her. Instead, she became efficient and brisk. 'All right, I'll drive you out to the airport. You can afford to fly—everything sold last night. Georgie's delighted, and you've got enough money to buy some really rare and exotic glazes. Finish that coffee and grab some toast and get packed while I organise your ticket.'

'I hate to leave you to deal with Wolfe.'

'Don't worry, I can cope with anyone,' Bobo boasted, adding slyly, 'I might even seduce him myself!'

Repressing a stab of violent jealousy, Rowan gave her a fake smile. 'Don't give him my address, please.' She waited tensely for the answer.

It came without hesitation. 'I won't,' Bobo promised.

Three weeks later, eyeing an ominous, murky sky, Wolfe murmured sardonically, 'An appropriate setting, Rowan—wild and extraordinarily beautiful.'

Had he been superstitious he might have wondered at the furious flash of lightning that spiked from cloud to cloud when he said her name. But he wasn't superstitious, and as thunder rolled and reverberated around the horizon he was too busy wrestling the yacht through another vicious squall to concern himself with lighting effects.

According to the chart he should be—yes, there it was, the fold in the bush-covered hills and the twist of the channel that indicated the winding, dangerous entrance to Rowan's hideaway.

Controlling a wheel made almost unmanageable by the gale that powered the slashing rain, he eased the craft into the opening, keeping an alert eye for wind changes and currents and rocks. Such risky sailing exhilarated him, but not into rashness, although when the harbour opened out before him he permitted himself a tight, hard smile of aggressive satisfaction.

The rain stopped as suddenly as it had begun, allowing a fugitive sun to bathe sea and coast in a sullen green glow. Shaking the water from his hair, Wolfe turned the bow into the wind before leaving the wheel to drop the mainsail. Under jib alone the craft slipped across leaden water towards a beach, bone-white beneath the violent sky. Almost directly ahead, set back from the rim of a low, tree-covered cliff, crouched a house, small and old and badly in need of a coat of paint.

Rowan's home.

From the corner of his eye Wolfe caught movement on the beach. Yes—even at this distance he recognised her, striding out of the grove of pohutukawas that bordered the beach. He narrowed his eyes, noting the dog at her heels and the shotgun over her arm. A sardonic smile curved his mouth. So the passionate, seductive ceramic artist had been out shooting. Rabbits, probably, as it was evening. Her confidence with the gun was another nail in the edifice he was beginning to build around her.

She hadn't taken two strides when she saw the yacht. Without checking she turned with the fluid grace that still starred in his hungry dreams and disappeared into the shelter of the trees, leaving the beach echoing and empty.

Wolfe smiled again, fancying he could feel her angry resentment blast across the water to strike him with fierce, elemental force.

But this time she wasn't going to get away from him.

When another round of thunder muttered behind the sombre hills, Wolfe took a quick glance at the chart and brought the yacht up into the wind. Like the lady she was, *Circe* responded instantly to his skilled handling, and within seconds he had the jib furled and the anchor down.

His skin prickled in the uncanny, age-old signal that warned him he was still under surveillance. Working to secure the yacht, he thought of the bowl he'd bought at the gallery—number 47.

Its subtle restraint reached some untouched part of him. Somehow Rowan had worked clay on the wheel to create an intense emotional experience.

To his own ironic astonishment, Wolfe had paid the very high price and installed the bowl in his home, where it gleamed like some rare and precious artefact, reminding him every time he saw it that the woman who'd made it had been responsible for his brother's death—and, through that, his mother's decline.

Rowan Corbett might be a genius with clay and the woman whose passionate response had damned near robbed him of his wits, but she was also the next best thing to a murderess.

Which made his own total lack of control where she was concerned all the more irresponsible. Especially as he'd had Tony's tragedy to forewarn him.

He suspected that she'd known who he was. Tony had been insecure enough to boast about his brother, and her abrupt departure was suspicious, as was her agent's shiftiness when he'd asked her for Rowan's address.

So she made love like an innocent houri; it would be interesting to see whether she'd deliberately used her beautiful body to soften him up.

If she had, she'd underestimated him badly.

It wouldn't be the first time a woman had made love to him with an ulterior motive, although he'd never before been hit by this lethal combination of rage and frustration and contempt both for her and for himself. He was armed against it now; he wouldn't fall again into the honeyed trap of sexuality.

Satisfied that the sea-bed provided good holding, he released the anchor warp and went down the three steps into the cabin, where he picked up a set of military field-glasses and surveyed the house.

Old, steep-roofed, with a verandah clinging to the front, it huddled behind the huge pohutukawa trees that clung with belligerent tenacity to the cliff-face, their long fibrous roots washed by the spray.

On either side of the headland curved two small beaches, pale semicircles reverberating in the uncanny, intense light. A third, larger bay swung away to the south, clogged with sinister grey-green mangroves.

If the land had ever been farmed it had defeated the settlers; fringed by more pohutukawas, primal bush brooded against the shore and clad the hills behind. After a swift, keen survey, Wolfe returned his gaze to the place where Rowan had disappeared.

A flash of movement saw him swing his glasses towards the other end of the beach. Yes, there she was, the big dark German Shepherd trotting at her heels as she headed towards a small boathouse at the base of the cliff.

An unexpected surge of adrenalin kicked him in the stomach, contracting his muscles for a split second, pouring unruly power through him. He disciplined it, smiling humourlessly as he tossed the field-glasses onto the upholstered seat and went back up into the dramatic turmoil of the day.

Thunderclouds massed again on the horizon, sharpening the sulphurous quality of the light, but the wind had dropped, leaving the air oppressively still. He lifted his face to the sky, satisfying some profound inner compulsion in a silent communion with the unfettered forces of nature.

An alien intensity jagged through his nerves and his sinews. Of course this wasn't some manifestation of Rowan's surveillance, yet it took all of his concentration to stay still, not to swivel and exchange stare for stare with the woman who watched him from the shelter of the trees.

He remembered the shape and size of her eyes, remembered their unusual, glowing colour—gold and copper and bronze, set in lashes and brows the same sable as her hair.

Remembered the look in her eyes when she'd lifted those heavy, slumbrous eyelids and said his name with him buried deep in her slim, tantalising body...

No wonder Tony had become obsessed by the seductive bewitchment of those eyes and that mouth. Wolfe controlled the stir of forbidden sexuality in his groin; Rowan's eyes hid dangerous secrets, but now that he understood the extent of her power he was armoured against her.

Three days before he'd seen Laura Simpson's doctor, who had said simply, 'I don't have anything more to offer. We have tried everything.'

'But there's nothing physically wrong with her?'

The doctor had shifted uncomfortably in his chair. 'We don't know that. We do know that we can't find anything physically wrong, but ME is not easy to diagnose, and stress is hugely important in managing it.' He'd looked at Wolfe's hard face and added, 'She's not likely to die.'

Brutally Wolfe had said, 'She might as well be dead. She used to be vibrant and happy, eager to get up each day. Now everything is such a huge effort that she's giving up.'

As he pulled on the painter of the small, inflatable dinghy that bobbed behind the yacht, and climbed down into it, he knew that whatever it took, whatever he needed to do—even if he had to kidnap Rowan Corbett—she was going to meet his mother and give her the information she so desperately needed.

By the time he reached the beach she was walking towards him, German Shepherd at her heels, both woman and dog bristling with antagonism. No sign of the gun. She'd probably stashed it in the boatshed.

Smiling humourlessly, he remembered her claimed prowess in martial arts. It would take more than a few fancy throws for her to deal with him.

More thunder was on its way, but for several moments spring was at her fickle and flirtatious best. The uncanny green light had transmuted into summery kindness, gilding the sand, transforming the water to glimmering turquoise, and illuminating the residual rain on the bush so that it glittered silver, like an enchanted forest.

Magnificent, but he wasn't here to enjoy the scenery—any scenery. Welcoming the splash of water around his legs, Wolfe stepped out of the dinghy just before it grounded. As he grabbed the rope and hauled the little inflatable up onto the sand the big dog barked and surged towards him, its raised ears and drawn-back lips an unmistakable signal of aggression. In one flowing movement Wolfe turned sideways to minimise his bulk. He could deal with the dog.

'Heel,' Rowan said sharply, her eyes enormous in her white face.

Reluctantly the dog returned to her, settling into its correct place. Although its gaze never left Wolfe's face he was satisfied it wasn't malevolent. No pit-bull intransigence there; the dog was simply doing what it had been trained to do—protect its mistress.

With a cold, fierce, anticipatory pleasure, Wolfe stopped where he was, forcing her to come up to him. He was establishing an advantage—something he needed, he admitted. His gut clenched, resisting a ferocious charge of pure sexual energy.

She'd lost weight, although her long, superb legs, narrow waist and full breasts were concealed beneath a faded, clay-spattered sweatshirt and trousers in a mustard shade that turned her eyes to pure gold. A gust of wind whipped a lock of hair across a face finer-boned than it had been three weeks ago.

Wolfe was assailed by a searing, white-hot memory of himself lying naked with that black hair around him in a clinging mass of silk, its texture and the slender heat and smoothness of Rowan's lush body drowning him in sensory overload while her sultry lips...

Stop right there! he ordered, clamping down on his rioting reactions until he was once more fully in command of himself.

Pacing behind her, the dog's lips lifted to show large, efficient teeth as though he recognised the trend of Wolfe's thoughts.

In an undertone Rowan ordered, '*Stay,*' as she came
to a halt about three metres away, her heart jumping with
a complex mixture of panic, joy and sheer shock.

Wolfe Talamantes had courage. Most men confronted
by Lobo in aggressive mode did their best to get out of
the way. Although he'd moved to minimise his size, and
therefore his threat to the dog, the cool assurance in his
stance told Rowan he was confident he could deal with
Lobo.

Had he found out who she was? A slither of apprehension iced her spine but she met his eyes fearlessly.
'What do you want?'

'That talk you ran out on.' He watched her with flat,
unreadable eyes.

Rowan's pulses motored into overdrive. As the fickle
sun disappeared behind another cloud, she mastered her
agitation enough to say, 'I haven't got anything to say
to you. I thought I'd made that plain.'

'I wonder what made you think I was so easy to get
rid of. I've got a lot to say to you.'

A frown pleated her brows. She didn't know him in
this mood—formidable, enrobed in a menacing energy
that set off alarm bells. For three weeks she'd gone over
every moment they'd spent together, even fantasised
about their meeting again. In her imagination he'd listened when she'd told him of Tony's death, and he'd
understood her part in it.

Imagination made fools of everyone. Somehow he'd
found out who she was. Head erect, hoping that Bobo
hadn't told him, she said, 'No.'

Wolfe watched as, hackles raised and teeth bared,
Lobo nudged in front of her, a big beast both jealous
and more conscious than she of the danger the intruder
represented.

Given time, Wolfe thought, he could arrive at some sort of friendship with the dog. Friendship wasn't possible with Rowan, yet behind the icy barrier he sensed the secret signals of sexual awareness, signals his own body was responding to with damned inconvenient timing.

Driven by an inner demon, he said, 'Do you realise that you and your dog have identical colouring? Hair as black as the pits of hell, and eyes like tawny gems. Is he your familiar?' Later he'd try to work out what he'd been playing at, but for now the dilating darkness at the centre of her eyes was his reward.

'I don't find that amusing,' she said frigidly. 'Please leave.'

His answering smile was poised on the knife-edge of antagonism. 'Not until we've talked about old times,' he said gently.

She lost colour, her heavy eyelids hiding those amazing eyes. 'Old times?' White-lipped, she managed to dredge up enough self-command to return, 'I don't have anything to say to you.'

'Whereas I,' Wolfe said, walking towards her, 'have a lot to say to you, and you're going to listen.'

Low growls bursting from his throat, Lobo shook with angry defiance, but without a signal from Rowan he remained where he was.

'He's well trained,' Wolfe said, his gaze flicking up to imprison hers. 'Are you going to give him the command he's desperate to hear?'

Cold rage iced her voice. 'Not at the moment,' she said, biting out the words because she wouldn't be able to order Lobo to attack, and Wolfe knew it. 'I'll hear what you have to say first.'

Clearly, contemptuously, he asked, 'Why didn't you answer my mother's letter?'

CHAPTER FIVE

ROWAN'S stomach clenched as Wolfe searched her face with impenetrable eyes the hue of darkest jade, so densely coloured they were almost black. His merciless scrutiny stirred something deep inside her.

So he did know who she was, and there was no doubt about his feelings. Yet, although she'd expected him to echo his mother's attitude, it wounded her acutely to hear the undisguised condemnation in his tone.

Stiff with foreboding, she said steadily, 'I've already told Mrs Simpson what happened with—with your brother. I told her six years ago, and she didn't believe me. Not only did she not believe me, she blamed me entirely for his death. Why would I want to listen to her accusations again?'

'She didn't believe you because your story of not see-ing anything was too convenient,' Wolfe told her bluntly, 'like your father's illness and inability to give evidence at the inquest.'

'He did give evidence,' she said steadily. 'It was writ-ten, but it was taken by the coroner in the presence of my father's superior officer.'

'Both of whom were good friends of his,' Wolfe said caustically. 'And who knew he was dying.'

Ignoring this because it was true, Rowan lifted her head. 'As for his illness being convenient, he died a couple of weeks after the inquest.'

'I know.' But his tone revealed no sympathy, no un-derstanding. 'My mother asked me to tell you she no longer blames you. I doubt if she ever did. She was shattered by Tony's death, and she intensely regrets taking her anger and misery out on you. And she needs to know the truth because she's very ill.'

Shame riveted Rowan to the spot as she remembered the lined, weary face of the woman she'd seen in the hotel foyer, and the white hair that had been dark at the inquest. She said hoarsely, 'I'm so sorry.' What had Mrs Simpson been doing in the hotel? Waiting for Wolfe? No, she'd been with a group…

'Will that change your mind?' When she hesitated, he answered himself with cold, cutting contempt, 'No, it won't. I suppose there's no reason why you should care about her.'

'That's emotional blackmail,' Rowan retorted stormily.

'It's the truth,' he said, stony-faced, watching her with narrowed eyes.

'It would be useless seeing her because I've got nothing else to add, nothing new to tell her. Please go away.' Her breath rasped in her lungs as she swung on her heel and started along the beach, desperate to leave him behind.

Growling another threat of defiance, Lobo stayed put, reluctantly following only when she called him.

With harsh distinctness Wolfe said, 'I'm not leaving, Rowan. We have unfinished business, you and I.'

As if to back up his statement, more thunder drummed beyond the horizon. Rowan turned slowly.

Collectedly she replied, 'You are, of course, perfectly within your rights to shelter here. You were lucky you found your way into the bay. Perhaps in future you'd better listen for the weather forecast. This can be a dangerous coast.'

'That almost sounded,' he said with smooth insolence, 'like a warning.'

In a tone that went from curt to frigid she said, 'The warning was in the forecast.' Once again she began to walk away.

'I've reviewed the evidence you gave at the inquest,' he said, the rasp in his voice more pronounced, 'and I believe there are enough discrepancies in your story to allow for the police to open the file again.'

Rowan stopped in mid-stride. God, she thought in anguish, would this nightmare never end? She'd been so sure she'd found sanctuary—and now it had been breached by this very powerful, dangerous man. What malicious fate had conspired to bring him to her exhibition at Georgie's?

But it wasn't fate that had driven her into his arms, or into his bed! She had to take responsibility for her own weakness.

Swivelling around, she demanded bitterly, 'Is that going to help your mother?'

The clouds rolled apart and through a rip in their sullen, seething fabric an unnatural light streamed onto him, highlighting the forceful, uncompromising features. A sombre, formidable figure in the midst of radiance, he waited like a keeper of the shadows.

For taut, terrifying moments Rowan stood transfixed, fighting off a clamorous impulse to run. Close at heel, Lobo growled again.

'Truth is always better than lies,' Wolfe said.

Still throbbing with profound dread, Rowan returned shortly, 'I'm very sorry your mother is so ill, but I can't help her in any way.' A complex mixture of anger and shame drove her to add, 'And I'm not going to sleep with you again, so there's nothing here for you.'

Lobo's growls erupted into angry barking that sawed across Rowan's strained nerves. 'Heel,' she commanded.

Wolfe hadn't moved. Coolly, scornfully, he said, 'I'm not going to touch you. You have one chance of avoiding that interview with my mother—you can tell me exactly what happened.'

Rowan flung over her shoulder, 'I don't have to answer any questions. And if I see you on my land again I'll charge you with harassment and trespassing. Stalking is illegal in New Zealand now.'

She strode off, marching back to the boatshed with straight back and head held high, getting almost to the bottom of the cliff before she heard the *burr* of the outboard's engine.

In the shelter of the trees she abandoned any attempt at dignity to race up the narrow path of twisted roots, Lobo hard on her heels. Only when she was close to the house did she stop; with her clenched fist pressed to her heart she watched the dinghy arrive at the sleek yacht.

At least, she thought, he hadn't known who she was the night they met; she couldn't have borne that. It would have been the ultimate humiliation if he'd made love to her in the hope of getting information from her.

She turned swiftly away and went into the house, muttering to Lobo, 'It's all right. He's nothing. He can't do anything.'

Even as she said it she knew she was wrong. Tall, broad-shouldered, with his dark, unwavering gaze and broken nose, his mocking, confident smile and sexy, determined voice, Wolfe Talamantes was very definitely someone—a dangerous, determined someone with the power to make her life even more a hell than his half-brother, because he knew far more about her than Tony ever had.

Sidelined panic kicked her in the stomach, turning her brain to jelly. Although she could keep him off the beach, she couldn't make him haul anchor and leave the little harbour. He'd found out her address and followed her up from Auckland—was it all going to start again? Did stalking run in families?

'Don't be so bloody ridiculous!' she said explosively.

A couple of loving swipes from Lobo's tongue as she wiped the sand from his paws comforted her a little, but she had to use gritty determination to shake off her unease. She filled a glass with water and stood staring into it for a moment before drinking.

Then, still buzzing with the adrenalin overload, she went out into the garden. She'd already staked everything against the storm—besides, she wanted to attack, not support. Crouching, she began to haul out weeds from a row of lettuce seedlings. Had Wolfe's threat to go to the police been empty? But even with the thought barely formed in her mind she shook her head. He didn't make empty threats.

For years she'd repressed the memories, kept them at bay with her work and the various jobs she'd taken to keep food in her cupboards—jobs that usually involved such hard work that she was able to sleep at night.

Would he leave her alone if she told him that Tony had stalked her, made her life hideous with threats and surveillance?

She yanked a clump of puha from between the lettuces. 'He wouldn't believe it,' she said flatly.

And why should he? Her friends hadn't; they'd admired Tony's bombardment of flowers and expensive presents, phone calls and cards and letters, not comprehending how stifled she'd been by the unremitting

weight of his obsession. Even her own father, a policeman, hadn't understood until too late.

Lobo wagged his tail and yawned, showing his splen-
did set of teeth.

'Fat lot of good you did,' she accused. 'Talk about a
washout as a guard dog!'

His grin always lifted her heart, but this time she
couldn't respond. The memories she'd tried so hard to
ignore came storming to the surface again, each bearing
its load of pain.

What would she do if Wolfe stirred up enough mud
to force the police to reopen the files? It wasn't just her
father's reputation she had to defend. His superior,
who'd been wonderful in spite of suspecting there was
more to Tony's death than she or her father were prepared to admit, was still in the force. He didn't deserve
to suffer for his loyalty.

Biting her lip, she attacked a dandelion.

'All I have to do is stick to the story,' she said out
loud. 'There's no new evidence, so they can't shake me.'

Lobo snorted.

Sitting back on her heels, she tried to smile. 'I wonder
if I chose you because you're black and tawny like me.'

The dog came over and pushed his head against her
shoulder. Obscurely comforted, she gave him a hug as
she stood up. 'No, when you tilted your head to look me
over, and then sat carefully on my foot and gave a funny
little baby growl at your brothers and sisters, I knew you
were the one.'

Grabbing the wheelbarrow's handles, she steered it
between the garden beds and tipped the weeds into the
compost bin. After putting the barrow in the car port
beside her elderly and fairly reliable motor scooter, she
had time to kill half a dozen large snails that were trying

to demolish the silver beet before rain pounced again and drove her indoors.

Hours later, dressed for bed, she looked out at a light on the water, small and dim—a watchful, threatening eye in her bay.

If she told Wolfe about his brother's harassment, would he realise how frightening it had been, or would he simply see it as the overreaction of a lovestruck man? Tony hadn't said much about his older brother, had never mentioned his name, but the tone of his voice had indicated love and a certain awe.

And Wolfe would have loved his younger brother. He certainly loved his mother. Shivering, she recalled the cold purposefulness in his words, his attitude—and, inevitably, the way he'd made love to her with such fire and passion.

Why did he have to be Tony's half-brother?

That night she dreamed again, the old dream where a laughing Tony shot her, and woke calling out, with Lobo whining and her face wet with tears.

It had been years since she'd been pitched back into her own private nightmare. She stumbled into the bathroom and waited for the tap to run warm.

'It was only a dream,' she reassured Lobo as he pushed against her.

But was it about to start again?

At least there were now laws against stalking, but Wolfe was powerful—no, the police would have to act if she filed a complaint. She washed her face, trying to banish the dream.

It didn't work. Still shaky, she decided she was in desperate need of a cup of tea, but in her chilly little kitchen, with its window out onto the harbour, she hesitated, letting her hand fall to her side instead of switching on the light.

'As though he'd be awake!' she said aloud. However, she made the tea in the fitful light of a sulky moon.

And when it was poured she took it into the dark sitting room and stood at the window. Growling, Lobo got to his feet and paced across to stand beside her, staring down towards the beach as lightning seared the sky.

Rowan quelled a sudden start, because she could see in the bilious flash that there was nothing—nobody—on the beach.

'Possums again, I suppose,' she said to the dog, who looked alertly around for the little animals he knew were enemies.

It was ridiculous to make Wolfe into a devil. Granted, he was a man with an effortless charisma that surrounded him like an aura, but he *was* only a man.

Into her memory there sneaked an image of the way the muscles in his back had flexed beneath the thin material of his shirt when he bent to pull in the dinghy. Rhythmically, smoothly, they had bunched and relaxed, shattering something knotted in the pit of her stomach.

She said through gritted teeth, 'If he comes above high-water mark again I'll send him on his way with a charge of pellets in his backside. Size five!'

That was when she remembered the shotgun she'd left in the boatshed.

'Oh, *bloody hell*,' she moaned, furious with herself for neglecting that most basic precaution.

She'd have to go down right now and get it. The combination of salt and dampness wouldn't be doing the weapon any good, and it was stupid to leave a gun where anyone could pick it up. Her hand stole up to her heart as more memories invaded her mind.

Aloud she said, 'No one will pick it up because no one knows it's there.'

But her father had trained her to unload any gun and put it safely away, and to hide the ammunition.

She cast a swift glance at the window. Usually she loved her view, but tonight the crouching trees and sable water vibrated with unseen horrors.

No! She'd worked hard to overcome her fear of the night, and she wasn't going to let Wolfe Talamantes stir it to life again.

Aggressively setting her jaw, she pulled on jeans and a warm sweatshirt and got into her gumboots. If anyone touched her, Lobo would attack. And, looked at with the cold eyes of logic, the only person likely to be prowling around was Wolfe, and he certainly wanted her alive so that she could talk to his mother. She'd be perfectly safe.

The dog an eager black shadow at her heel, she set off. She could feel his alertness as they slipped beneath the pohutukawa trees and picked their way down the cliff path, illuminated by the moody moon and flashes of lightning from behind the hills.

Inside the boatshed the darkness closed around her in a stifling heaviness. Aiming the torch at the ground, Rowan switched it on. Water glimmered like obsidian, still and shiny, and she could see the blue-black gleam of the shotgun barrel along the joist where she'd left it.

Jolted by relief, she put the torch on the joist and was reaching for the gun when Lobo erupted with a fusillade of barking and leapt towards the entrance, vanishing into the night.

Heart skidding, Rowan snatched up the shotgun and swung around, leaving the torch pointing towards the entrance. Dimly recalling various thrillers she'd read, she scurried sideways as far as she could out of the narrow beam of light.

Above the frantic pumping of her pulses she heard a confident male voice command Lobo to 'Stay!' Lobo barked furiously, but clearly he wasn't attacking.

Shock and paranoia roared into action, fuelling an angry reaction that hovered perilously on the edge of panic.

She took a deep breath and steadied her voice to call, 'Lobo! Here!'

Still barking, the dog backed around the end of the boathouse into the torch beam. Although Rowan had both gun and dog for protection, the sight of Wolfe's tall, hard-edged silhouette brought back a sickening burst of memories that swamped everything but the primitive compulsion to run. Frozen by fear, she scrabbled desperately for control.

A fierce light dazzled her as he trained his torch onto her face. Blinking, she shook her head.

'Put down the gun,' Wolfe ordered calmly, but the crack of authority in his tone jerked her out of her terrified trance.

Remembering too late her father's stern injunction never to point even a toy gun at a person, she dragged a breath into her aching lungs and lowered the barrel towards the ground. Growling, Lobo raced down to stand with her. The torch moved closer.

'Stay there,' she said thinly.

'Put down the gun.'

Rowan didn't move. 'I feel safer if I keep it where it is.'

'I've got the cartridges.'

Hot rage pumped through her, lending her a spurious feeling of control—rage with herself for being so stupid as to leave them there, and fury with him. 'Give them back to me right now.'

'Not,' he said laconically, 'while you're in charge of a gun.'

It took all of her strength of mind to say roughly, 'Stealing as well as trespassing, Wolfe?'

The torch beam revealed a brief flash of white, humourless smile. 'I'll leave them where I found them when you've gone. I don't trust women who are as careless with guns as you are.'

'What the hell are you doing on my land? Besides snooping, of course?' she demanded scornfully, reining in her temper. In the face of his ice-cool composure, losing it would put her at a huge disadvantage.

'Just looking around,' he drawled.

He wasn't, she realised incredulously, even going to try to justify his presence there. Chilled by memories of another man who'd often appeared when she least expected it, she said dangerously, 'That's harassment. Any more and I'll call the police.' Briefly satisfied at the way his dark brows met above his nose, she added, 'And don't ever come back.'

'Presenting a weapon is also an offence,' he said on a flinty note that backed up his implied threat.

'You're trespassing!'

'That doesn't entitle you to wave a gun at me,' he said calmly. 'I'm going now. I'll see you tomorrow.'

Rowan bit back a stinging reply and watched silently as he stepped back into the devouring darkness of the night.

After automatically checking to make sure that no cartridge was in the barrel, she held the shotgun on the point of balance while she switched off the torch. With Lobo in front of her she stood for several minutes until her eyes grew accustomed to the lack of light, then made her way to the entrance, looking around carefully.

Nothing moved. Out in the harbour the light at the top of the mast still glowed like an angry eye. No other light showed; no engine broke the silence. Somewhere out there Wolfe watched and waited.

Old terror, old fears, surged against the barrier she'd built against them. Silently cursing the man who'd re-awakened them, she walked up the cliff path.

In the house she locked the gun away and sat down on the edge of her bed, her heart thudding in her chest as though she'd narrowly escaped great peril.

'Pull yourself together,' she muttered.

She was being an idiot. Feeling oppressed by an all-pervading sense of Wolfe's presence was simply wallowing in unjustifiable melodrama.

'Think logically,' she told Lobo, who wagged his tail and gave her his endearing grin.

She got up and walked across to her bedroom window, staring down at the small spark in the darkness. Snooping could be a prelude to stalking; Tony had spied on her.

'Of course the tendency to stalk doesn't run in families,' she said briskly as a squall flung itself on the house, tossing the huge branches of the trees about so that the light from the yacht seemed to blink on and off.

Wolfe was making himself objectionable because he wanted something from her, something specific and logical.

But then, so had Tony—she stopped that thought before it had time to form, ruthlessly dragging her mind back to Wolfe and his dark, handsome face and that overpowering aura of potent male sexuality. Fine tremors pulled her skin tight as she remembered just how potent...

Her first glance at him had hurled her into a place where the rules no longer applied. Common sense had flown out the window, replaced by an exaggerated blend of excitement and abandon.

But she had to overcome that, return to her normal cautious self. She couldn't tell Wolfe what had happened. It wasn't just her secret.

Shuddering, she let the curtain fall. 'Anyway, it won't help his mother,' she said to the impersonal night, walking slowly back to her bed as she recalled Mrs Simpson—elegant, beautiful, distraught—who was now desperately ill.

Telling her the truth would probably kill her.

Rowan woke slowly and reluctantly, only to leap out of bed when she saw the clock. 'Quick, Lobo, quick—it'll have to be a short walk this morning,' she called.

In fact they had time only for a run down the cliff to the boathouse. Yes, Wolfe had left the cartridges on the joist where she'd stowed the gun. Biting her lip, she stuffed them into the pocket of her jeans, and without looking at the yacht threw sticks for Lobo to chase along the beach, apologising to him for cutting his playtime short.

Even so, she reached the café ten minutes late, earning a sour look from the owner. 'What happened?'

'Sorry, I overslept.'

'Well, you can work it off at lunchtime. We've already got a customer.'

Pinning a smile to her lips, Rowan collected her pad and pen and went out into the cheerfully fuggy room.

And met a pair of burnished green eyes. Wolfe's eyes.

Her stomach launched itself into freefall. 'Good morning,' she said, struggling to sound normal. 'What can I get you?'

'Poached eggs on toast, bacon, and grilled tomatoes,' he said coolly. 'And coffee.'

'Espresso?' she asked, deliberately distancing herself from the night she'd given in to the same rage of passion that was tearing at her now. Of course he drank black coffee, strong as sin and packing a huge punch.

One dark brow twitched upwards. 'Naturally,' he said laconically. 'Why adulterate the caffeine with additives?'

Rowan's smile surprised her. As well as angering her and shocking her and making her feel like a wanton, this man could amuse her. And that made her even more wary.

When she carried the coffee out he asked lazily, 'Do you enjoy working here?'

She gave him a meaningless smile. 'It's great for people-watching,' she said, not trying to hide the sting beneath the words.

Had he realised that she worked here when he decided to come in for breakfast? Possibly. In three weeks he could find out almost everything he needed to know about her. A cold shiver snaked its way down her spine.

Fortunately a couple of regulars came in then; she left him to take their orders, but as the café filled she was aware of Wolfe's eyes on her, and the way the other customers glanced at him from the corners of their eyes.

That mysterious thing called presence alerted them to the fact that he was someone important and interesting. Or perhaps it was his face and bearing; in spite of his blazing good looks, the strong bone structure of his face and the gleaming green eyes, the arrogant twist of his mouth, proclaimed him a man to be wary of.

Of course his build might have something to do with it—she'd read that tall people had an automatic advantage over short people, and beneath his casual, well-cut clothes Wolfe's big, seasoned body proclaimed strength and power.

No, she thought, seeing him in her mind. He was simply the dominant male.

'Rowan!'

She started as the owner snapped at her. 'Coming,' she said, smiling determinedly as she went to the hatch. She couldn't afford to lose this job until she'd had at least one more exhibition.

'Stop drooling and do some work.'

Rowan's smile faltered, but she picked up the tray and took it out into the café. Wolfe had heard the insulting comment; she'd seen his lips tighten.

Not much later he left, leaving her to wonder how on earth he'd got there.

At two o'clock she rode home on her motorised scooter, took an ebullient Lobo for a run through the sodden bush, and then retired to the shed that was her workshop. Refusing staunchly to glance out the window, she sat down at the wheel, calling up every ounce of self-command to free her mind of images of the man who owned the yacht.

Stubbornly she formed beakers, easy, ordinary things that still needed concentration. Potting was not for those who couldn't control their hands and their minds.

As dusk was closing in Lobo got to his feet and paced across to the window, staring with fierce attention through it. After a moment he whined and came back to stand beside her, staring up with restless, tawny eyes.

'All right, boy,' Rowan said, her voice even, 'I know he's still there.'

The German Shepherd went to nudge her hand with his nose.

'No,' she said sharply, and, reminded that he wasn't to touch her when she was at the wheel, he sat down and watched, intelligent face alert. She made him wait until she'd finished throwing the pot and cut the base with wire. Only then, as the wheel ran down, did she get reluctantly to her feet and walk over to the window, rubbing a hand across the back of her neck.

She shared her dog's uneasiness. A warning stronger than logic, more primitive and unconfined, rasped through her.

'Cabin fever,' she explained to Lobo, who had followed and was staring with her out into the rain. The faint outline of the yacht coalesced through the murk, pitching in the waves. Wryly she said, 'I hope he doesn't get seasick. And what's he doing in a yacht like that, anyway? Billionaires buy thumping great super-yachts, with crews to do all the work and stabilisers to keep their stomachs happy, not sleek, graceful racing yachts.'

The familiar little sound of Lobo's snort made her laugh. She stooped to ruffle his thick, coarse mane. 'It won't last; it'll blow itself out, you'll see, and he'll get sick of beating his head against a brick wall and sail away. Then we'll race down to the beach, and you might just be able to catch a seagull.'

But Wolfe had no intention of leaving. Like a predator he planned to hunt down his prey until he found exactly the right moment to strike.

'Except that he can't do anything,' Rowan said aloud. 'All I have to do is stay calm and not let him rattle me.'

Barking, Lobo leapt to his feet, twisting to face the door. Chilled, Rowan swivelled to follow his gaze.

A tall, formidable figure was walking out from beneath the pohutukawas onto her lawn. Even in jeans and a thick woollen jersey beneath a bright yellow slicker, Wolfe looked worldly and self-assured and very, very dangerous.

Rowan stiffened her shoulders against the panic that hollowed her stomach and numbed her brain. 'Round two, or perhaps three,' she said, pitching her voice so that Lobo wouldn't pick up the icy slither of fear down her spine. 'Well, we knew he'd be back. Let's go out and meet him, shall we?'

Ashamed because for a fleeting second she'd wished she wasn't wearing an elderly sweatshirt and stretch leggings, both splotched with clay, she closed the door of the shed behind her.

They met under the car port behind the house; this time Lobo barked with recognition that held a note of warning.

'Quiet,' Rowan said automatically, adding when the dog fell silent, 'What do you want?'

'I need to talk to you properly,' Wolfe said, his flinty face uncompromising.

'I think we've said everything that needs to be said.'

'No. Ask me in.'

It was close enough to a command, yet the request weakened her resistance. Tony had never asked...

'What will you do if I say no?' she challenged.

He shrugged. 'Keep trying.'

'Until you wear me down?'

His eyes narrowed. In a cold, gravelly voice he said brusquely, 'Until I convince you that I'm not here to

cause any trouble. All I want from you is that you let
my mother know the truth.'

Mind churning, Rowan looked away. So the night
they'd spent together meant nothing to him compared to
his mother's illness. Although the brutal rejection
clubbed her emotions into stupor, some part of her relaxed. He was hounding her, yes, but she sensed he was
telling the truth.

Tony's seemingly lightweight persona had masked a
chilling, determined selfishness. Wolfe was doing this
for his mother.

Yet she didn't dare believe him entirely. She warned,
'You're wasting your time.'

'I'll be the judge of that.'

She hesitated, then shrugged and opened the door into
the dank laundry that served as the back entrance. 'All
right, come in,' she said ungraciously.

Picking up the dog's towel, she bent to dry his wet
paws, muttering crossly when he jigged around, trying
to keep Wolfe in his sights. With Lobo clean, she
washed her hands in the concrete tub. Wolfe had hung
his coat on the hook by the door and was taking off his
shoes; once she'd shucked hers, she led the way through
the kitchen into the small front room.

It smelt musty and damp; after suggesting he sit down
in the only comfortable chair she possessed, she busied
herself lighting the fire, standing when it had caught to
find Lobo watching Wolfe warily.

'He's a magnificent beast,' Wolfe remarked. 'How old
is he?'

'Three years.' Gingerly she sat down on the sofa,
avoiding the broken springs. The burning wood crackled
and spat, sending shadows dancing up the wall. Lobo

lay deliberately down beside her and put his head on his paws.

Warning signals ringing, she pleated a bronze and green fold of the Indonesian throw rug and said abruptly, 'What do you want?'

'Why the hell are you working in that café?'

'I have to eat, and so does Lobo,' she shot back.

He leaned back into the chair, watching her with half-closed eyes. The firelight played warmly over her face, and she looked away from that intent gaze.

He asked, 'Couldn't you find anything more lucrative?'

'Not here.' She folded her lips tightly together, clamping them on the words that wanted to tumble out.

'And why do you have to live here?'

'I don't consider that any of your business,' she said scathingly.

'Everything about you is my business at the moment,' he said, with a smooth insolence that didn't hide a truly intimidating determination.

CHAPTER SIX

WHEN Rowan flinched, Wolfe said sharply, 'What's the matter?'

'I don't like threats.'

His mouth hardened. 'I'm not threatening you.' At her disbelieving glance he stated, 'All my mother wants is to know the truth. She won't take it any further—and neither will I, if that's what's worrying you. This is solely for her peace of mind.' He paused, then added, 'And perhaps to save her life. She seems to have reached a point where she doesn't care whether she lives or dies.'

Excellent tactics—first the threat, then the promise, followed by an appeal to her better self. 'But she knows,' Rowan told him, striving to sound reasonable. 'She was at the inquest—she heard what happened…'

'At the time she was too grief-stricken to take much in,' he said grimly.

But not too grief-stricken to accuse a shattered Rowan of her son's death.

Wolfe went on, 'She managed to pick up the pieces of her life, but Tony's death broke her heart. She needs to know—and so do I—why you and your father connived at a cock-and-bull story that had Tony waving a gun around so carelessly he accidentally shot himself. Tony knew about firearms; he was always careful with them.'

The lamp by the chair threw his reflection onto the wall like an eighteenth century silhouette. Apart from the chiselled mouth and the slight bump in his nose there were no curves in that profile, Rowan noted as apprehension kicked beneath her ribs. It was all angles and straight lines—a compelling, forceful indication of his character.

She said levelly, 'I'm terribly sorry for your mother, and I know how this must hurt her, and you, but I don't have anything new to tell either of you.'

Wolfe's mouth compressed. 'So explain to me what happened. You met Tony at a party at Cooksville, where you lived—a party thrown by friends of yours?'

'Yes.' She had to stop herself from squirming under his cold, judicial survey.

'He was very attracted?'

Alarm prickled across her skin. 'We both were,' she admitted reluctantly. 'He seemed a nice man.'

'Good-looking and rich.' Not quite a sneer.

At first hot then icy under Wolfe's merciless survey, Rowan knew she couldn't afford to give way to outrage and anger. She traced the pattern in the fabric on the arm of the sofa and said colourlessly, 'Good-looking, yes. I didn't know the state of his bank balance. I wasn't interested.'

'You've changed,' he said with a wounding flick of contempt. When she glanced up in surprise he added, 'You certainly knew who I was. Why else did your agent drag you away if it wasn't to fill you in on the state of my bank balance?'

Rowan flushed, folding her lips tightly.

Reverting back to that cool, intimidating tone, he said, 'You and Tony went out several times together—parties, barbecues, the usual summer events at a tourist place.'

Rowan nodded. She'd been flattered when Tony had tried to sweep her off her feet; only native caution had kept her firmly upright.

'At the end of the holidays he went back to Auckland, and you followed him for your first year of university—'

'I didn't *follow* him,' she interrupted. 'I was already enrolled at the School of Fine Arts.' He knew all this. He was deliberately taking her through it like a detective intent on catching her out.

Well, she was a policeman's daughter.

Wolfe's brows lifted. 'But you went out together.'

'On and off for a couple of months,' she told him. 'It wasn't an intense relationship. We didn't—' She stopped, colour licking along her cheekbones.

'You weren't lovers,' Tony's half-brother said conversationally, although green fire glittered beneath his thick lashes.

Rowan swallowed, made hot by the fierce energy of his attention. 'As you know,' she retorted, not hiding the acid in her tone.

'So you kept him dangling.' When she refused to fill in the deliberate pause he drawled, 'That was clever of you. He was used to women who succumbed immediately. Why did you hold him off?'

'I have no intention of explaining my motivations to you,' she returned evenly, sickened by his implication that she was a cold-hearted tease.

'You have no intention of explaining anything to me.' The unsparing words slashed through her composure.

'Exactly.' She met his gaze with proud defiance. Lobo's head came up. The dog looked from one to the other, then settled to watch Wolfe.

He ignored the animal. 'At the end of the first semester you went back home to Cooksville and he followed, and asked you to marry him.'

'Yes.' Her tone was subdued, but she kept her head high.

'You refused.'

'Yes.'

His mouth tightened. He exuded an indomitable strength, a kind of primal forcefulness that made her shiver. Cold eyes marked that involuntary response.

Lobo growled and surged upward.

'Down,' she commanded, and watched the dog closely until he settled back, his hackles still proclaiming his wariness.

'Why?' Wolfe asked.

'Because I didn't love him,' she said without a tremor.

An unknown emotion splintered the enigmatic depths of his eyes into blazing shards of crystal. His eyelids veiled the transformation before Rowan could fully register the effect it had on her stomach, a sudden lift and drop into nothingness. She'd felt that way when she'd bungee-jumped, dazzled, terrified, and so excited she couldn't do anything but feel—as though the centre no longer held and infinity stretched around her.

Unsparingly Wolfe proceeded, 'That weekend he followed you home to Cooksville, went out pistol shooting on the range with your father, came home with him, quarrelled with you, and brandished the pistol he'd carried in for your father—a pistol with a bullet still in it.' In a voice heavily laced with sarcasm he finished, 'Then somehow, without meaning to, he shot himself.'

Praying he wouldn't notice how much effort it took, she parried his gaze with an assertive chin and a composed face. 'Yes.'

'Just like that,' he said, so silkily precise his comment overloaded her nerves with icy electricity. 'Why was he so angry? He'd been seeing other women during that semester.'

Clinically he noted her teeth clamp on her lip, the

haste with which she folded her long hands in her lap to hide their sudden tremor, and the quick upwards glance from blank, enamelled eyes. 'I know.'

No doubt her father had taught her how to deal with interrogation. Say as little as possible and stick to your story. Why did this woman, of all the women he'd met in his life, have the power to shatter his self-control? He said roughly, 'Tony's reaction seems extreme—almost bizarre.'

'Yes,' she agreed, her flat, opaque gaze defying him to probe further.

But Rowan Corbett was a woman who provoked extreme, bizarre reactions—a temptress with eyes of fire, a face that would haunt him until he died, and skin like satin made flesh—a woman who left an imprint on a man's soul.

Was this how Tony had felt?

Wolfe's frustrated fury sought release in action—violent, savage, mindless. He leashed it, but each word emerged with lethal impact. 'And you don't give a damn, do you?'

After a considered moment she said bleakly, 'Of course I care. I thought—think—he must have reached some sort of snapping point, but I don't know what it was.'

She was lying. Yesterday, when he'd told her he didn't believe her story, she hadn't blinked, had shown no sign of surprise or indignation. Today she'd had the same reaction: no umbrage at being called a liar, just a dogged, minimal defence of her actions.

Wolfe knew he was considered a hard man with an uncanny ability to get results. Most of his success was due to good planning and the capacity to make the best use of every twist and turn of circumstance; some of it was his ability to calm volatile situations and raging antagonists.

No volatility here, and no aggression, but he didn't fool himself that Rowan was as calm as she seemed to be. He could sense anger smouldering beneath her disciplined detachment. Anger—and fear.

So he had to ignore the impact of her sultry, beckoning eyes and sensuous mouth, ignore the erotic memories and play this through to the end.

He said, 'I don't believe he asked you to marry him.'

Avoiding his eyes, she shrugged. Her long fingers reached for the dog's head, caressed the ears, sank into the heavy ruff.

Banishing a fleeting, arousing image of those hands in his hair, across his chest, curving around his hips to bring him closer, Wolfe said with cold, concentrated scorn, 'In fact, I don't believe a word you're saying.' He got to his feet in a rapid, easy movement and reached for her shoulders, fingers tightening to draw her off the sofa.

Her eyes widened. Ignoring Lobo's low growl, he searched for something he knew he wouldn't find in the tawny golden depths. She knew how to keep her secrets. The tip of her tongue touched her lips, and in spite of everything Wolfe enjoyed a fierce, primitive satisfaction because she didn't say the words that would set the bristling dog onto him.

Rowan flinched and tried to pull away, but his hands tightened around her upper arms, strangely gentle although she could feel the curbed power drumming through him. It summoned a wildness in her that she hated and feared.

His eyes clashed with hers in a brutal challenge. 'You see, I know that after the inquest you went back to university and handed in a paper that got you another A. Remarkably cold-blooded, I thought.'

Shutting down her responses, her thoughts, she stared at him with a blank expression.

After a taut, white-hot moment he dropped his hands as though she contaminated his skin, and stepped back.

Lobo burst into loud barking.

'Quiet!' Wolfe commanded, waiting until the dog subsided into silence before saying laconically, 'Which makes me even more interested in what really happened that afternoon. As well, I want to know why you ran off to Japan so soon after the inquest. Almost as though you had something to hide.'

'I can tell you why.' Her rusty voice rasped her throat. 'Because my father had just died, and thanks to your mother's outburst I couldn't go anywhere without the media poking a camera in my face. There was nothing in New Zealand for me.'

'So you packed your genius in your backpack and ran away.'

In spite of his scathing tone her heart leapt at his offhand acknowledgment of her talent. Cold with dismay, she realised again how dangerous it was to be so vulnerable to a man she actively disliked and had good reason to fear—a man whose every glance, every intonation, set untamed sensations jangling through her.

Rain lashed the side window, driven in from the sea by a howling gust. Rowan said abruptly, 'If you want to get back to your yacht you'd better go now. It's already dark and I think a storm's building.'

He followed her glance and said something succinct and unheard under his breath before walking over to the door. Once there he turned and said with icy, assured menace, 'I'll go now, but it's not over, Rowan. I'll find out exactly what happened if I have to take you apart to do it.'

Shaken, her stomach knotting, she asked, 'What made you decide to start this up now? Why wait so long after Tony's death?'

His raised brows denied her the right to ask this question, but he said coolly, 'We found you.'

The words hung in the air, raising the hairs on the back of Rowan's neck as another blast of wind shook the house. Dry-mouthed, she said, 'I see.'

'I hope you do. If the only way for my mother to regain her health and her will to live is for her to understand exactly what happened, I'll do whatever I need to do to force you to tell her.'

Rowan's heart clenched. Understanding his grief, however, didn't mean she was going to give in. He thought she had no compassion; so be it. She met Wolfe's measuring gaze with brittle defiance. 'Why don't you get married and give her some grandchildren to live for?'

The moment she said the words she knew she'd crossed some invisible line. His expression hardened into a tough, unyielding mask. 'She needs to know the truth,' he said in a voice that almost blistered her skin. 'And it's personal now.'

'Eventually you'll have to go back to being a billionaire,' she said, concealing a very real pang of fear beneath a scornful tone.

'That won't let you off the hook. I have a reputation for getting what I want. And I want this very much.'

His hooded gaze seared her skin, burned into her brain so that she couldn't think, summoned instant heat from that treacherous part of her that wanted him. She blurted inanely, 'Will you be able to get back to your boat in this?'

Although Wolfe looked tough enough to deal with anything the universe threw at him, even he had to be vulnerable to the forces of nature.

'I won't drown, Rowan, much as that might please you.'

'I don't want you drowning off my beach!' she snapped.

'Why? Afraid of killing another man?'

She went white. 'Is that what you think? That I killed your brother?'

He paused, dark eyes gleaming and pitiless as they scanned her face. 'I don't know,' he said slowly. 'Not yet.'

Rowan's skin tightened. 'Why is it so impossible to believe that he—?' Her voice died under his flinty gaze. She swallowed and went on, 'That it was an accident?'

'Because—unlike you—he'd been taught to be careful with guns. Tony would never have carried one without unloading it, or waved one around so wildly that he shot himself accidentally. And he wouldn't have slipped—he was like a cat on his feet.'

Using all her energy to hide her apprehension, Rowan said, 'It was an accident. I told him that it was over and he—he just lost it. He grabbed the gun, and then—'

She stopped, her voice cracking in her throat, sweat dampening her temples.

Wolfe looked like a bronze statue except for the cold, flat, greenstone eyes. When she refused to go any further he supplied caustically, 'And then he tripped and shot himself in the heart. Think up another story, Rowan; that one might have worked in Cooksville, where your father was respected and his superior was complaisant, but I don't believe a word of it.'

She swallowed again and said thinly, 'It happened.'

'It's a lie,' Wolfe said softly against the keening of the wind around the windows. 'One I'm going to break. And if I have to break you to get to the truth, I'll do that too.'

He meant it. Rowan repressed a shiver of pure fear, before summoning the stamina to say, 'You're wasting your time and energy.' She heard the branches of the pohutukawas groan and creak as another gust of wind struck. Biting her lip, she said, 'You can't go out in this.'

'Are you offering me a bed for the night?' he asked with insolent familiarity.

'No! But there are motels in—'

'I have no transport, and there's no way that scooter of yours would take a passenger. And, no, I'm not going to borrow it.'

She demanded, 'How did you get into the café this morning?'

'I walked up the boundary between your land and your neighbour's,' he said curtly, 'and he offered me a ride in. And one back when I'd finished.'

Yes, that was Jim—the salt of the earth!

Wolfe added, 'I can manage this; my dinghy is built for rough weather.'

Rowan cast around for some way to ensure his safety that didn't involve him staying with her. None presented itself, and she said lamely, 'I'll come down with you.'

'Don't worry,' he said with aloof contempt. 'You don't have to see me off.'

'Not in the mood for snooping tonight?' Another thing better not to have been said.

He shrugged. 'Not tonight.'

'Lobo needs a walk,' she said, angling a stubborn chin.

'Forget it. It's too rough out there.'

She gave him a cool look. 'We're not made of icing sugar. Come on, boy.' Lobo's tail started wagging enthusiastically.

Wolfe said between his teeth, 'You're not going out in this.'

'You can't stop me,' Rowan pointed out, a spark of malice in her tone. 'If necessary we'll follow you down.'

He said violently, 'All right then, do what you damned well please.'

Triumphant as though she'd broken even in a tough fight, she put the fireguard in place and followed him out, closing the door behind her. While the two humans dragged on oilskins and boots Lobo pranced around, ears pricked and tail active at the prospect of a walk.

A lot of good he was as protection, Rowan thought acidly; he seemed to have yielded supremacy to Wolfe with some primal canine acceptance of an alpha male. Perhaps it was the name!

Miraculously, once they'd got into their wet weather gear the rain and wind snapped off, leaving behind an eerie silence broken only by the restless waves attacking the rocks at the base of the cliff. They weren't big enough to be dangerous yet, but it wouldn't be long before they were.

'A window of opportunity,' Wolfe said sardonically, switching on his torch.

The beam cut through the darkness, hard-edged, conical, so bright that it wasn't worth Rowan using hers. At the top of the cliff path Wolfe took the lead, and Rowan wondered at this man, who suspected her and despised her, yet automatically went ahead to protect her from falling.

'Where's your dinghy?' she asked.

'In the boathouse.'

He'd tied it to one of the pegs beside the steps that led down into the black water slurping against the piles and planking.

With Lobo at her heels Rowan switched on her torch and directed it onto the dinghy. Perhaps she should suggest he stay…

Are you *mad*? she asked herself, hardening her heart. Watching him bring the yacht into the harbour had been an education in brilliant sailing. He could certainly cope with this sea. She said crisply, 'I'll cast you off when you've started the engine.'

'Careful—gumboots are a hazard in the water.' Wolfe lowered himself into the sturdy craft with relaxed, powerful male grace.

More of that unthinking protectiveness. In spite of the antagonism sizzling through her, unwanted excitement twisted in the pit of Rowan's stomach as he bent to start the outboard. The beam of her torch wavered, catching Lobo stretched out on the decking, head on one side as he watched Wolfe.

'I don't plan to fall in,' she retorted.

'Make sure you don't,' Wolfe said, glancing up.

'Be careful,' she said impulsively, frowning. 'It might be dangerous out there. Are you sure you can handle it?'

Dark eyes gleamed suddenly, and the beam of light shifted again, pointing up the stark angles of his face. Stunned by the wildfire burst of sensation ricocheting through her, Rowan wished she could paint him like that, a study in gold and shades of darkness—a mythical, archetypal marauder out of every woman's dreams, both threatening and powerfully, compellingly attractive. Her bones melted in a primitive, feverish response.

'I can handle it,' he said evenly.

He lifted a hand; she stepped forward to cast him off. The outboard burst into raucous life, and the dinghy began to move towards the entrance.

Swiftly, angrily, Rowan turned away, a careless foot landing squarely on Lobo's tail; he yelped and tried to leap to his feet. Instinctively jerking sideways to avoid falling on him, Rowan pitched forward and into the water.

She had a mini-second to gulp in air and thrust her arms outwards before the water closed around her, dragging her down to the bottom as her gumboots filled. She wasted a few seconds trying to kick them off, giving up when they clung and refused to move. She'd drown before she got them free.

Fiercely resisting panic, she manoeuvred beneath the surface, heading for what she hoped to be the steps, hoping that Wolfe had heard Lobo yelp, that he'd seen her go down...

Self-preservation summoned her in an imperative voice; she fixed her mind on survival, opening her eyes to catch a smeary glimmer of light—Wolfe? Or the torch she'd dropped?

Whatever, she aimed desperately for it, using up precious energy to force her weighted feet along, doggedly pushing through the clinging, sapping water towards the light.

She knew after a few steps that she wasn't going to make it, but she kept going. I'm going to die, she thought dimly. I'm glad I made love with Wolfe...

Heart throbbing violently in her ears, and her lungs painfully compressed, she was almost ready to surrender to the temptation to gulp in water when a hand fastened onto her hair and hauled her up to the surface.

Gasping, choking, air whistling into her starved lungs, she heard Lobo's frantic barking, and the next moment felt his claws scrabbling at her shoulders.

'Stay!' Wolfe shouted, fending the dog off with one hand as his other swept across her back, anchoring under her armpit. He began to swim for the steps, followed by an anxious Lobo.

Rowan struggled to help, but already shock had her shivering and her arms and legs felt like lead. If it hadn't been for Wolfe's strength she'd have sunk again.

'Keep still,' he ordered in a harsh voice.

Thankfully she surrendered, letting him do all the work. Once they reached the steps, his shoulders and arms bunched as he boosted her up and onto the deck.

Gasping and retching, she collapsed onto the wooden planks, shuddering with cold and anger at herself for being so stupidly careless. Almost immediately she began to struggle up, but Wolfe's swearing and several splashes, followed by the slight give of the planks beneath her cheek, satisfied her that both he and the dog had made it out.

Lobo's warm tongue across her cheek brought her eyelids up. The torchlight wavered, dazzling her, but she could see the dog's narrow, intelligent face and hear him whine his concern. Behind him loomed a dark figure, water streaming from him.

'I'm all right,' she choked, and to her utter horror burst into tears.

'Don't try to get up yet,' Wolfe commanded above the dog's agitated barking. He knelt at her feet, yanking off her boots to empty them before easing them back on and standing up. 'Come on,' he said grimly, pitching his voice above another heavy shower and the moans and creaks of the old boathouse. 'Stop snivelling and start walking. Immersion hypothermia is best dealt with by vigorous activity.'

Ruthless hands lifted her to her feet and forced her along the planks. Rowan set her jaw and compelled her feet to move. If she was wet and cold, he was too, and so was Lobo.

'I c-can't have hypo—hypo...' Shivers racked her. She gritted her teeth to say weakly, 'I wasn't in the water long enough.'

'Long enough to damned near drown,' he said grimly, adding, 'And if we don't get back to the house straight away it won't be mild hypothermia either. Come on, get those feet moving up the steps.'

Even with the support of his arm and his strength, it took all of her energy to make it up the cliff, but at the back door she said through chattering teeth, 'I'll run a bath and while you have it I'll rub Lobo down.'

'Don't be an idiot,' he said roughly, pushing her through the door and beginning unfastening her oilskin. 'Your lips are going blue and you can't stop shivering, and your breathing is too shallow for my liking. Lobo's far better able to deal with this than either of us. I'll rub him down while you get under the shower.'

'I don't have a shower,' she said, clenching her jaw against the shivering that racked her.

'You have a bath, I hope?'

Surprised into a chuckle, she said, 'F-first on the left.'

He tugged the oilskin from her and half hauled her into the bathroom, where he turned on the taps over the old-fashioned, claw-footed bath, straightening up as she tried to drag her jersey over her head.

She made it, but it left her dangerously exhausted.

Still shivering, she plucked uselessly at the buttons on her shirt. Brushing her hands away, Wolfe unfastened it for her, his face impassive. At his touch, a complex mixture of embarrassment and shame and hunger prowled through her, underlaid by an astonishing, overpowering sense of security.

'Leave your underclothes on,' he said, unzipping her trousers and beginning to ease them down her legs.

· Rowan closed her eyes. Only the bitter knowledge that she wouldn't be able to undress herself kept her silent— that, and the constant shivering.

When she was standing in front of him in her bra and briefs he straightened up and turned away to test the bath water. 'That's fine,' he said. 'Can you get in?'

Golden eyes duelled with green. Rowan's will flagged and she said dully, 'I don't know.' Her voice sounded strangled and she wasn't sure she could move.

Silently he picked her up, enveloping her in the heat of his body for as long as it took to lower her into the water. 'All right?' he asked. 'Can you sit up?'

'Yes, th-thank you.' Touched by his concern, she relaxed into the delicious comfort.

'The water's not too hot?'

'N-no, it's wonderful.'

'I'll rub Lobo down and then make you a hot drink,' he said over his shoulder, leaving the door open behind him.

The warmth found its way right through her lax body and into her bones. She lay for what seemed ages, listening to the rumble of Wolfe's voice as he talked to Lobo. He knew about dogs; his voice was deep with affection and understanding, which was possibly why Lobo liked him.

Once she stopped shivering she forced herself to her

feet, clutching the taps for support but determined to get out. Wolfe was also wet, and by now he'd be starting to feel very cold.

'Get back in,' he commanded from the door.

She stumbled; he caught her before she hit the bath.

'Sit down,' he said, and such was the ring of authority in his voice that she found herself in the water again.

'I'm not Lobo,' she flared, 'and I'm not shivering any more. It's your turn—you must be freezing.'

She glanced up and realised that he'd found the hot water cupboard in the laundry and looted it. Instead of his wet clothes he wore a huge old woollen jersey that had been her father's, and had wrapped a blanket beneath his arms.

He should have looked funny. He didn't. He looked barbaric and invincible.

'I'm warm enough,' he said, his even tone not hiding the steel beneath as he surveyed her face. 'I've been stoking the fire. Stay there until you've drunk the cocoa.'

He disappeared, returning before her sluggish brain had time to formulate a sensible reply.

'Can you manage it?' he asked, setting the mug down on the edge of the bath. 'I'll hold it for you if you can't.'

Rowan was not going to let him feed cocoa to her. Gritting her teeth, she reached out a white hand and lifted the surprisingly heavy mug to her lips. It was hot and rich and thick, and it tasted like nectar.

'Drink the whole lot,' Wolfe ordered.

'Yes, *sir*.'

He grinned, lights dancing in his eyes for a second before they shut down and he turned away.

He was at the door when she said, 'Lobo—'

'Is hosed down and drying off in front of the fire,' he told her, and walked out.

Rowan drank the cocoa down to the dregs before forcing her leaden legs to carry her out of the bath. Taking off her bra and briefs almost exhausted her, but she dried herself sketchily and then wrapped the towel around beneath her shoulders, hoping it hid the essential parts but too tired to care much.

She heard Wolfe moving around in the kitchen. It took her two attempts before she could call, 'The bath's free now. The towels are in the hot water cupboard,' and walk into her room.

He followed her. 'Are you dry?' he demanded from the doorway, eyes scanning her face.

'Yes!' She glared at him, daring him to say anything more.

There was an electric heartbeat of silence, before he nodded and turned away. 'There's tea in the kitchen. Drink at least two cups of it in front of the fire. No alcohol.'

'There isn't any in the house,' she said to the empty doorway.

Slowly and creakily, she pulled on an elderly pair of tan trousers and a jersey the same tawny-gold as her eyes. After some frustrating minutes brushing her hair, she pulled it back from her face with a tie and set off towards the bathroom, carrying the man's green dressing gown that always hung on the back of her bedroom door.

'Come in,' Wolfe called in answer to her tentative knock.

He was standing with a towel knotted around narrow hips, his wet clothes tossed with hers into the empty bath. Too much skin, she thought dizzily, coppery and smooth and gleaming with dampness, each taut swell of muscle and sinew a profound statement of strength and masculine potency. Shoulders that loomed, and a pattern of hair spearing downwards to disappear beneath the folds of the towel; overpoweringly and uncompromisingly male, Wolfe dominated the room and her thoughts, sending jagged pangs of excitement through her.

Quick colour scorching her skin, Rowan held out the dressing gown. 'This should fit you,' she said woodenly.

Before taking the robe, he surveyed her with unwavering eyes for a leisurely, unbearable moment, before asking, 'Who does it belong to?'

CHAPTER SEVEN

ROWAN understood how her dog felt—baffled, resentful and suspicious, yet unable to resist Wolfe. His green eyes mesmerised her. She felt that if he tried he'd be able to pry her thoughts from the innermost recesses of her brain. Angrily, she lifted a mutinous face and met the icy brilliance of his gaze with stubborn defiance.

'It's none of your business,' she said without expression, 'but as it happens it was my father's.'

He took it from her. 'How do you feel?'

'A bit tired,' she admitted.

'You're stronger than you look.'

She stooped to pick up the wet heap of clothes, his and hers intermingled, wondering at her reluctance to touch them. Such extreme reactions were not normal for her—but then, meeting Wolfe had transformed her into another woman, one whose turbulent emotions kept threatening to break down the fragile armour of her control.

He commanded, 'Leave those. I'll deal with them.'

'I'll put them on to wash. The sooner they get in front of the fire the sooner they'll be dry.'

'In front of the fire is where you're going right now,' he said grimly. 'I've built it up again. I'll put the clothes in the washing machine.'

'I can—'

'Just get in there and sit down,' he interrupted, 'before I pick you up and carry you there.'

'Oh, *all right*,' she said stonily, backing out.

Collapsing onto the sofa in the sitting room, her fingers buried in Lobo's dark ruff, Rowan accepted bleakly that the only way to banish Wolfe from her life before he permanently damaged it would be to tell him what he wanted to know.

If she didn't, he'd keep pushing until his patience and temper snapped, and then he'd carry through on the threats he'd made.

But she couldn't tell him. And as the night they'd spent together clearly meant nothing to him, she couldn't allow it to mean anything to her—not that, nor Mrs Simpson's anguish.

Guilt at this thought clenched her hand in Lobo's fur. He made a questioning sound and blinked at her.

'Sorry,' she said, her voice catching in her throat as she rubbed around his ears in the particular way he loved.

Should she contact her father's superior, the man who'd tacitly made it possible for them to cover up the circumstances of Tony's death? No, of course she couldn't! He was a policeman, and if she told him what had really happened he'd be forced to investigate, especially when Wolfe began to press him.

Because if he couldn't get anything from her, Wolfe would dig deeper; he'd found her, and it would be much less difficult to find her father's superior officer, now much higher in the police force after six years.

All she had to do was stick to her story and again learn to live with a conscience that had always pricked her. Taking meagre comfort from the fact that telling Mrs Simpson what Tony had tried to do couldn't help her—would make her realise just how dangerous her beloved son had been—Rowan stilled her hand. Lobo pushed his head against her leg.

'Good boy,' she murmured.

He was still damp, but Wolfe had dried him down—
and brushed him too, by the look of him. Which meant
that Lobo had trusted him enough to let him handle him.

Or that, like her, Lobo had had no choice. She looked
at the big dog with a cynical smile. 'Pathetically helpless
against him, both of us,' she said beneath her breath.

Somehow, without knowing it, she'd become—no, not
dependent on Wolfe, but vulnerable to him in a way
even more frightening than the fierce physical attraction
that still shocked her. She stared into the flames, trying
to work out how he'd managed to penetrate her defences.
Of course she wasn't in love with him—it didn't happen
that fast.

But apart from that acute, passionate awareness, she
liked him in lots of ways. She even admired his determination…

She was balanced on the horns of a dilemma—convince Wolfe that he was wrong about Tony's death and
she'd never see him again; fail to convince him and he'd
carry out his threats, ruthlessly staining the career of a
man whose only fault had been to stand by her dying
father.

Both prospects were unbearable.

Her hand stole to her breast; terrified, she listened to
the rapid skip of her heart. No, she couldn't be falling
in love with Wolfe. No and no and no.

'I won't let it happen,' she whispered fiercely.

Yet her body sprang to life when Wolfe came through
the door carrying a tray, the arrogant angles of his face
clamped into an intriguing, invulnerable mask.

He'd retrieved milk from the battered refrigerator and
even found some sugar. Against the white tray and the

delicate glaze of a tea-set she'd thrown years ago his hands looked dark and boldly male.

You are not, Rowan told herself trenchantly over the buzzing in her ears, going to give in to this humiliating craving. It will pass.

It has to pass...

It was impossible to read the thoughts behind his impassive face, those hooded eyes. His glance speared hers before dropping to her hands.

'I'm not shivering any more,' she said, holding them out so that he could see their steadiness.

'And your lips are a normal colour again.' There was a disturbing intimacy in the way he scrutinised her mouth. 'How's your breathing?' he asked, setting the tray down beside her.

Rowan reached for the teapot and concentrated on pouring, careful not to touch the spot on her hand where she'd pulled out a splinter. 'Perfectly normal.'

Which was a lie. She felt as though she'd been punched in the stomach. Scent, she thought violently, had to be the most evocative of all the senses. When he'd put down the tray he'd been close enough for his faint fragrance—masculine, incredibly arousing—to set up an instant clamour inside her.

Struggling to regain control of her voice and her mind, she said, 'If you like cake, there's some in the tin in the pantry.'

'I'll get it,' he said, and left the room.

Rowan put down the teapot. Her father had been a big man, but the green dressing gown strained at Wolfe's shoulders and reached to just above his knees.

Men, she'd always thought, looked mildly ridiculous in dressing gowns. The most handsome actor tended to go from sexy to boyish when he donned a dressing gown.

This man hadn't. The sombre green towelling that filled his startling eyes with shadows made him more tough and forbidding. Hastily, before she could head down that dangerous path again, Rowan began to pour the second cup of tea as he came back into the room with several slices of cake on a plate.

She put the teapot down and looked up at him. Coaxing the words past a raw patch in her throat, she said, 'Thank you for saving my life.'

'You'd have made it out if your damned dog hadn't tried to drown you first,' he told her, sitting down in the chair.

'He's not much good as a lifesaver,' she agreed, adding soberly, 'And I wouldn't have made it—I was just about to pass out when you grabbed my hair. I'd have breathed in water, and then I'd have drowned. So— thank you. I'm grateful.'

'You wouldn't have felt obliged to see me off if I hadn't been prowling around the night before.' Leashed anger roughened his tone. 'Hauling you up was the least I could do.'

It wasn't exactly an apology, especially as he followed it with a cold, uncompromising smile. 'Besides, you haven't yet told me what I want to know. As for Lobo, he might be no great shakes as a lifesaver, but he barked loudly enough to carry above the sound of the outboard.' He reached out and ruffled Lobo's ears. The dog accepted the caress with dignity.

'So he should have,' Rowan said, ignoring the threat. 'I fell over him!' She picked up the milk jug. 'Do you like your tea adulterated?'

'No,' he said, smiling with a hint of mockery.

'We'd both better have sugar. It's good for hypothermia and shock.' Not that Wolfe seemed to be suffering from either. 'Two spoons, I think.'

He didn't object, so she ladled the sugar in. He was watching her closely, however, and when he'd accepted the mug he said, 'How do you feel?'

'Oh, I'm fine.' She gave a brief smile. 'The bath worked wonders. How about you?'

He shrugged. 'No problems. But then, I wasn't anywhere near drowning.'

Rowan bit her lip and drank some tea. 'I was getting desperate,' she admitted.

'Not,' he said grimly, 'half as desperate as I was, believe me. It's going to be a long time before I forget the sight of you falling into the water and Lobo going berserk before jumping in after you.'

Rowan shivered. 'It was such a stupid accident. I tried to twist sideways so I didn't land on him, and lost my balance.'

'I assumed it was something like that.' He glanced at the dog. 'He was doing his best to reach you. I had to push him away before I could haul you up.'

'Thank you,' Rowan said. 'He'd have done his best, but I don't think he'd have got there. It's quite deep in the boathouse, and he's not strong enough to haul me up.'

Wolfe got up and crouched in front of the fire, deftly adding a chunk of driftwood from the basket at the side. Multi-coloured flames flickered higher, seizing greedily on the dry, salty wood. Lobo sat up to watch Wolfe's strong, skilful hands feed in another couple of logs, stacking the fire for maximum heat.

The tea tasted of nothing in Rowan's mouth. It seemed hours since they'd left the room to go out into the night; everything felt different, as though she'd walked through an invisible door into another dimension. She felt different too—a new person, altered in subtle, immutable ways.

Amazing, she thought with a flash of acerbic irony, what a dunking and a fright can do to you!

When Wolfe resumed his place on the sofa Rowan offered him the plate. 'Have some cake.'

'Thank you.' He took a piece and bit into it. 'I don't recall having tasted a cake with feijoas in it before,' he said, referring to the oval green fruit with scented, sweetly tart flesh that grew in every Northlander's garden. 'It's delicious. Did you make it?' When she nodded he said casually, 'An unusual skill amongst women of your age.'

What did he know about ordinary people's lives? Rowan thought trenchantly, taking a slice of the moist cake. Lobo looked up eagerly, although good manners forbade him to beg.

Sedately she said, 'My grandmother was a wonderful cook. She taught me how to bake. It's Lobo's and my besetting sin. I never ice cakes, though. That would be decadent.' She divided her slice and dropped the larger portion into Lobo's waiting mouth.

One of Wolfe's brows rose with lethal effect. Rowan thought of Regency rakes—sophisticated, deadly dangerous and showing a confidence so inborn it approached arrogance, yet with a sharp, subtle sense of humour and a rock-hard code of conduct.

'And whatever you are,' he said evenly, 'you're not decadent.'

'You have a problem with that?'

His long black lashes lay straight and dense for a second on the tanned skin above his high cheekbones. They lifted to reveal a cool, guarded glance that rebuffed her as conclusively as an acid comment. 'Seductive teasing is a cold, naked exercise in power. That comes pretty close to decadence for me.'

Sickened and startled by the open attack, Rowan put her cake down. 'If you're referring to your brother—'

'Who else would I be referring to?' His scathing tone flayed her composure.

Proudly, because pride was all she could summon, she resumed, 'I didn't tease him.'

'Going out with him, telling him you loved him and then dumping him wasn't a tease?'

She said quietly, 'So no one should ever change their mind? Where is it said that a few evenings together constitute a lifetime commitment?'

'Nowhere,' he said curtly. 'You're twisting my words.'

A soft growl from Lobo turned both their heads. 'It's all right,' Rowan said automatically. She looked at Wolfe, speaking with passionate intensity. 'I went out with Tony for two months. I don't know how he felt, but the word "love" was never spoken by either of us in those months.' She pushed the bad memories into the furthest part of her mind, the part where demons gibbered and mouthed. 'And he didn't love me. He—' She stopped.

'He—?' Wolfe drawled, watching her with hard, narrowed eyes.

'He assumed too much, too quickly,' she said bluntly, her stomach churning. She couldn't eat; instead of leaving the half slice of cake, she unthinkingly fed it to Lobo, and realised the moment it disappeared behind his teeth that she'd revealed her inner turmoil.

Unable to stop herself, she shot a swift glance at the man opposite.

Wolfe's gaze lingered on the dog, then flicked up to her face with the impact of a sword. 'In what way?'

'In every way,' she said shortly.

She expected a further inquisition, and was relieved when he said as he picked up his tea, 'Did you make these?'

'The mugs?' Rowan asked. 'Yes.'

'They're good,' he said calmly.

'I know.' She stretched out to pick up her own.

'What have you done to your hand?' he demanded, getting to his feet. 'Show me.'

He didn't wait for permission; long fingers enclosed hers and turned her hand over so that he could examine the palm.

'It's all right. It's just a splinter.' She had to force the words through a tight throat.

Which closed completely when sensation exploded through her, accelerating her heartbeat until time spun out, suspending her in a void. Staring helplessly at their joined hands, she tried to control the fire summoned by his touch.

Lobo growled again as she jerked her hand free.

What's happening? What have I done? she thought, panicking. Thinly, she added, 'It must have come from the decking.'

'Have you put anything on it?'

'Yes. Some antiseptic ointment.'

Frowning, he relinquished her hand and sat back on the sofa. Lobo relaxed, but kept an eye on him as he picked up the mug and drank from it, setting it down to say, 'Keep an eye on it. Splinters can infect,'

'I'll make sure it doesn't,' she said crisply, and added,

'Your mother brought you up to be very protective of women.'

'She brought me up to be considerate of anyone weaker than I am.' His voice was coolly reflective and his eyes gleamed as he added, 'I don't include you in that category.'

It was both a declaration of war and a back-handed compliment. 'I'm gratified,' she said in her driest voice, and added, hoping that her reluctance wasn't too obvious, 'You can't go back to the yacht. And I haven't got a drier, so it'll take all night for your clothes to dry in front of the fire.'

Turning his head, he looked through the window. Rain drummed across the roof, hiding a moment of tension, of awareness so acute that Rowan thought she could feel his presence with every cell in her body.

After a moment he asked evenly, 'Are you suggesting I stay here?'

'You'll have to,' she replied in her most composed voice, ignoring the outcry from her instinct of self-preservation. Hastily she added, 'I have a spare room.'

Wolfe's lashes drooped. 'In that case,' he said with masterly irony, 'I'll accept, thank you.'

Jerkily Rowan stood up and moved towards the door. 'I'll get Lobo his dinner and then start on ours.'

'Show me the spare bedroom,' Wolfe said, 'and I'll make the bed. And then we'll both cook dinner.' His tone made it clear that that wasn't an option; she was going to have him working in her small, shabby kitchen, like it or not.

She did not like it. He took up more space than his size entitled him to. 'It will be simpler if I do it myself.'

'Not tonight. You're exhausted.'

Although Rowan had stopped shivering, her limbs still

weighed heavy, but the tiredness gripping her went beyond the physical. Surrendering to his stronger will—just this time! she promised herself—she said, 'I'm not, but thank you for offering,' and walked rapidly through the door. She needed time for her foolish heart to ease back to a reasonably steady beat.

After she'd pointed out the spare bedroom and told Wolfe where the sheets were, she said, 'Come on, Lobo. Dinner.'

The dog pranced off beside her, but even as she tipped into his dish a large chunk of the meat loaf loaded with rice and vegetables that she cooked specially for him, his attention remained fixed through the door and along the hall.

Rowan knew how Lobo felt. If she closed her eyes she could see Wolfe Talamantes imprinted on her lids—his handsome, autocratic face and lean, honed strength, the arrogant, disciplined authority, the lithe animal grace based on co-ordination and total confidence.

For the past weeks she'd tried desperately to forget him—to forget everything about the night they met—without success. Every second of that meeting was imprinted on her brain, a necessary and essential part of her. She felt connected to him, as though their wild lovemaking had forged a link that transcended the physical.

It scared her witless.

Perhaps, she rationalised, rinsing out the container in the sink, it was her old, abandoned love sculpture calling her. The memory of Wolfe's tanned, magnificent body still had the power to tighten her gut in instinctive homage. A passion, not connected to the sexual delight he'd given her, itched to immortalise it. Perhaps if she did, she'd be free of this acute vulnerability.

A clay model first...

No, he'd never pose. And how could she do justice to his eyes, keenly intelligent, overwhelming his hard features—eyes that saw too much, knew too many secrets about her, and wanted to know more…?

Shaken by exquisite need, she wondered why she'd asked him to stay instead of ringing Jim, who'd have taken him into the village.

Except that it was hardly fair to Jim. And it was only one night. With Lobo she'd be perfectly safe. Even without Lobo she'd be safe! The years she'd spent learning to defend herself meant she could deal with any situation that threatened physical harm.

Anyway, she was almost certain there was nothing unstable about Wolfe. Hard and ruthless, yes, but he wasn't like his brother—the threat he represented was to her peace of mind, not her life.

Or was that another example of wishful thinking?

Rain drummed with staccato insistence on the roof as she left Lobo to his food and checked the washing machine, its subdued banging and thumping informing her that it had almost reached the end of its cycle.

Instead of seeing to dinner, she lingered in the chilly laundry. Light from the windows revealed pohutukawa trees tossed in the wind, their heavy, sinuous branches clawing at the air, leathery leaves flicking to reveal the silver underside. Bunches of buds whipped like chained snowflakes across the blackness beyond.

In December, when the land and the sea were at their warmest, Wolfe would be long gone and those buds would open to reveal scarlet and crimson flowers like small brushes—so many that when they fell they'd stain the water beneath the cliffs the colour of blood…

Rowan swallowed. Lobo paced through the door and pressed against her, his warm shaggy body tense yet comforting. After a day when her life seemed to have been turned on its head, she needed comfort.

She was torn with sympathy for Laura Simpson, who'd given up on life because of a hunger for the truth—a truth that would shatter for ever her illusions about her dead son.

Trust her, Rowan thought bleakly as she opened a cupboard door and took out a folding clothes horse, to lose her head over a man who had the power to make her life as much a hell as his half-brother had.

She carried the clothes horse down the hall and into the sitting room. Wolfe stood in the window, frowning down at the harbour. He swivelled as she came in, and came across, saying abruptly, 'I could have done that.'

'It's not heavy,' she said, relinquishing the metal frame to him and watching as he set it up—a tricky job that had him swearing beneath his breath as it collapsed.

When Rowan laughed he glanced up with gleaming eyes. She stopped, her mouth drying. Two deft movements from Wolfe had the clothes horse under control.

Straightening up, he said bluntly, 'You don't have to fetch and carry for me, Rowan. I'll get my clothes from the machine and hang them up.'

'All right, although they're not quite finished yet.'

As rain spattered across the windows, he glanced back.

Divining what was worrying him, Rowan said, 'Your yacht will be all right. It's good holding out there, and she's actually more sheltered than we are.'

'I know.'

Hoping to lighten the atmosphere, she asked, 'What made you call her after the enchantress who turned Ulysses's men into pigs? Surely that was asking for trouble?'

Amusement glinted behind his lashes. 'Don't forget that Circe fell in love with Ulysses.'

'A dangerous woman, nevertheless,' she said brightly.

He gave her a cool, mocking glance. 'The world is full of them, but I can handle that.'

She'd bet there was very little Wolfe couldn't handle, especially when it came to women. A jagged thrust of some forbidden emotion took her by surprise.

'What did I say?' he asked, those piercing eyes intent.

Shrugging, she said, 'You strike me as being the competent sort.'

It seemed important that he not recognise her evasion for what it was, but although she made her eyes wide and innocent she couldn't tell whether she'd succeeded.

'Having second thoughts about offering me a sanctuary for the night?' he asked, watching her with dispassionate aloofness.

'No!' She answered too swiftly, too emphatically, and had to follow it with a more neutral, 'Not at all. I'm just not used to guests. Even in summer the harbour entrance is so tricky that few people find their way in, and once they've seen Lobo they usually find their way out again.'

'And you don't relish any intrusion on your privacy,' he finished, and sent her a calculated smile of such potent, compelling charm that it heated her bones and smoothed over her tension like honey melting across pancakes, eclipsing her fierce self-preservation with an equally old, subtly stronger instinct.

But in spite of her body's treacherous desire to surrender, her cynical mind applauded. He'd tried intimidation, and that hadn't worked. Now it seemed he was going to try seducing the information he wanted from her.

It hurt because she was beginning to want much more

from him than sex, but she could cope. It would take more than flattery and charm to persuade her secrets from her.

'It makes me sound churlish—and reclusive—but, yes, you're right,' she said. 'And I do have to keep working. I'm a potter with orders to fulfil.'

'Why settle in this out-of-the-way spot?' His voice was casual, as was the glance accompanying it, but Rowan knew by now that with Wolfe there were no unimportant questions.

Equally casually she replied, 'My grandparents lived here. Because of my father's job we moved around a lot, so this was always home.'

'If you sold it,' he said idly, 'you could probably buy a much more modern place closer to town, with enough left over so you wouldn't have to work. Land like this, so private and with such beautiful views, is worth a small fortune.'

'I like it here, and so far I've managed.' Shrugging, she changed the subject without finesse. 'I'll go and start dinner.'

He gave her a keen glance, and got to his feet.

While she sliced a previously roasted pepper into strips and added them and some herbs to the leaves torn from her small planting of lettuces, he washed the new potatoes, then shelled broad beans. Rowan prepared the spears of asparagus before making up a dressing with balsamic vinegar and extra virgin olive oil. He was deft and quick, a man who needed to be shown something only once.

And he seemed to take up all the room in the kitchen, so that whenever she moved she found him right where she wanted to be. Every so often they accidentally brushed against each other, sparking off a forbidden response in every cell in her body.

'These are the last of the broad beans,' she said when the atmosphere began to prickle with tension. 'They hate the hot weather.'

'Changeover time,' he said laconically. 'The end of one season and the beginning of another.'

Her skin tightened in a primal warning.

'Tell me where the utensils are and I'll set the table,' Wolfe said, startling her.

He wouldn't understand how reluctant she was to let him into her cupboards and drawers; he'd probably never looked in his own. No doubt he had a housekeeper, and he'd certainly possess the very best of linen and cutlery.

'I'll do it,' she said quickly.

When he frowned, she suspected that he understood her feelings, and flushed.

He said, 'Put it on the bench and I'll take it through. Where do you eat?'

She opened a drawer and took out the only decent tablecloth she possessed. 'On the small table in the sitting room. It's more comfortable than the dining room, which is freezing if I don't light the fire.'

As soon as he'd disappeared with the cloth she rapidly got out knives and forks, salt, pepper and plates, glad that when she'd arrived home the day before she'd rescued five trembling early rosebuds from the rain. They were now open; while Wolfe set the table she put them into a cut crystal vase that had belonged to her grandmother, and took them in.

Cream, with hearts of gold, they rested in the centre of the table like fragile, gauzy Victorian maids of honour, their lazy, provoking scent rising effortlessly above the more earthy, savoury smells of the food.

A few minutes after they'd begun dinner Wolfe commented, 'You have a multitude of talents—potter, cook, and gardener. Is there anything you can't do?'

'That's about all I *can* do. Don't ask me to sew or knit or run a computer.' Surprised and pleased by the compliment, Rowan forgot herself enough to smile without fencing it behind caution. The salad was tasty and crisp, and he was demolishing the tiny white new potatoes in their shroud of butter and chives with a speed that fell just short of greed.

'Working a computer doesn't require talent, just the ability to follow instructions and think logically.' He chewed another mouthful and commented, 'Kura Bay has an excellent butcher.'

She forked up a broad bean. 'Courtesy of my neighbour.'

'The gregarious and helpful Jim?'

Rowan smiled. 'I grow vegetables for him; he gives me meat and fish in exchange.'

'You don't have problems with 'possums?'

Rowan met his eyes coolly and dispassionately. 'I probably would if I didn't trap and shoot them.'

She hated doing it; she felt like a murderess. But it was worth it. No great trees held gaunt, dead limbs above the forest canopy on *her* land, and in summer the shore was ringed with fiery blossom, unlike the coasts to the north and south of her.

Fiercely she said, 'I wish our ancestors had left their wretched mammals at home!'

'They didn't know about ecology,' he said. 'Both Polynesians and Europeans were wanderers who moved into islands and continents without realising the harm they or their livestock could do. And, to be fair, it would have been impossible for the Europeans to keep out rats.'

'They didn't have to introduce anything else,' she said sternly.

'They suffered from a very human lack of imagination and understanding,' he said, and smiled when she snorted, his eyes reflecting greenly in the soft light above the table as his gaze lingered on her face. 'Aren't you lonely living here, miles from anyone but a man who apparently spends most of his time out fishing?'

Perhaps, but she found it safe too. She'd rather he kept on trying to bully her—at least that was honest—instead of turning that potent, experienced charm onto her.

'Lonely? Not a bit,' she said blandly.

'Is this your work?' he asked, nodding at the bowl she'd filled with fruit.

It was one of her favourites. The burnished glaze was easy to manipulate, but it looked spectacular. And the shape was almost perfect.

'Yes.'

His long-fingered hands touched it with a gentleness that sent a shiver down her spine. He'd touched her like that—gently, and then he hadn't been gentle at all...

Concentrating on her food, she locked and barred those treacherous memories.

'It's beautiful,' he said, as though he hated to admit it.

Rowan strove to squash a flickering, suspect joy. It wasn't the first time her work had been praised, yet his words meant so much more.

'I'm good at what I do,' she said prosaically.

'You're better than good—you're an artist,' he said with cool assurance.

'Thank you.' She picked up her half-empty water glass and sipped to ease her arid throat.

This house was her haven and her fortress. She wasn't

accustomed to having it invaded through the postern gate, and that, she told herself, was why she was feeling hot and languorous and edgy.

Rowan knew herself to be at a disadvantage. In her experience rich, sophisticated men were greedy and demanding, like children who chased butterflies, uncaring that their grabbing for beauty crushed wings and killed the object of their desire. Since Tony she'd avoided any entanglements, helped by five years of living like a nun in Japan.

However, she suspected that no amount of experience would have helped her deal with Wolfe; he didn't behave like any other man she'd met.

The night they'd spent together might mean nothing more to him than good sex, but for her it had been a transcendental experience, marking her in ways she was only just beginning to understand.

'You must be very fond of your own company,' he said, probing none too subtly.

'And Lobo's.'

Lobo lifted his head. He didn't growl, but his reserve was palpable.

'Named by a romantic,' Wolfe said, something akin to mockery underlying the words.

'I didn't call him that—his breeders did,' she told him defensively.

'He's a superb animal. Did you train him?'

'Yes,' she said serenely. 'Although he's pretty strong-minded he wanted to learn, so it was exhilarating even when he was stroppy. It took patience, but he was always eager; we got there.'

Wolfe's disturbing greenstone gaze scanned Lobo's dark face, then flicked up to Rowan's. 'A bit like you learning martial arts,' he said.

So he knew about that too. She said haughtily,
'You've been doing a lot of research.'

'I like to know as much about my adversaries as possible.' The steel in his voice sent chills along her spine.

CHAPTER EIGHT

'WISE of you,' Rowan returned crisply. 'Would you like some fruit and cheese? We can eat that with coffee in front of the fire. I'll see if I can find some crackers.'

'Stay there,' Wolfe told her. 'I'll find the crackers and cheese and make the coffee.' He got up, unconcerned that he was still only wearing her father's dressing gown.

But then he'd be well aware that, no matter what clothes he wore, his size and confidence and tough authority—that sense of power held firmly in check—produced a relentlessly male impact.

As much as Rowan despised herself for the involuntary reaction that ricocheted through her, she couldn't control it. Hastily she began stacking the plates.

Wolfe frowned. 'Go and sit by the fire. I'll take this stuff out.'

'I'm fine,' she said with a snap in her voice.

His hand closed around her wrist. 'Rowan,' he said, so quietly that ice scudded down her spine, 'sit down by the fire. You don't have to wait on me.'

Although he held her loosely, there was no denying the forcefulness in both his words and the loop of tanned fingers on her pale skin. To Rowan's chagrin her breasts throbbed and a provocative fire beaded her nipples.

Furious, she glared up into his face, but words dried on her tongue the moment their eyes clashed. Tiny and scintillating, the metallic flecks in his seemed to dance in the densely coloured matrix of the iris. Something swift and fierce and aching clutched the pit of Rowan's stomach before exploding like a supernova.

Twisting free as though she'd been scorched, she muttered, 'I'm not sick.'

'You're not up to par yet,' he said, letting her go to scoop up the dishes.

Rowan's breath locked in her lungs. 'I'm just a bit tired,' she stated, backing away, her body taut with hidden anticipation.

It was headlong retreat, and he knew it. Without a further glance he carried the dishes through the door—probably, Rowan thought drearily, amused.

No, it wasn't amusement she'd seen in his face. It had been desire, a dark flame that had stamped his autocratic features with primal hunger until he'd curbed it.

If only she could control her response so easily! Collapsing onto the sofa, she gulped in draughts of air as Lobo rubbed against her knee.

Nothing happened, she repeated like a mantra. You looked into his eyes, that's all. He grabbed your wrist. And, although your skin is still burning as though he's branded you, *nothing happened*.

If she said it often enough she might even convince herself it was true.

So why was her jaw so tightly clenched that the muscles in the back of her neck shouted a protest? And why did she feel that someone had applied a flame-thrower to the stuffing in her bones?

Lust, she thought, trying to be sophisticated about it—a simple matter of mindless, elemental chemistry. Instant and electrifying, it had overwhelmed her the instant she met Wolfe's eyes at the exhibition, and she'd been tipped so far off-balance she still hadn't recovered.

Except that if it was lust, why did she care so much what he thought of her?

Five minutes later, by the time Wolfe returned with coffee, crackers and cheese, she'd brought the fruit bowl across from the dining table, the small task lending her some composure. Her heart still thudded like a piston in her constricted chest, but at least her hand was steady when she accepted her cup, and she even managed a light, informal tone when she offered him fruit.

Wolfe surveyed the bowl of mandarins and oranges and oval shining tamarillos glowing as warmly as cabochon rubies. 'Aren't you going to have some?'

Her stomach knotted. 'I'm not hungry.'

He gave her another of those assessing glances, then selected a mandarin and deftly peeled it. Lobo's head came up, and after a speculative glance in the dog's direction Wolfe flicked a segment at him. It landed on his front paw.

Lobo's mouth visibly watered, but he sat staring at Rowan until she said, 'Eat, Lobo.' The small, brilliant crescent disappeared into the dog's mouth so quickly it seemed like a conjurer's trick.

Wolfe laughed quietly as a tail thumped the floor and Lobo did his best to look winsome. 'Will he eat for anyone else?'

'A few selected people.' And now for Wolfe, probably.

He picked up his coffee and leaned back in the chair, subtly making it his. 'Do you have to work at the café tomorrow?'

'Yes.'

His smile had an element of cynicism in it. He knew she wasn't going to proffer information. So, without finesse, he asked, 'Do you really enjoy working there?'

Rowan stared at the coffee in her cup, noting with a detached eye the faint tremors across the dark surface. 'I've told you, I like watching the people,' she admitted cautiously. 'And it gives me the afternoons and evenings for potting.'

'So that's your true career?'

She stated, 'It's not just a career, it's the most important thing in the world to me.'

His brows lifted. 'I see.'

The fire crackled and spat as another wave of rain exploded onto the corrugated iron roof. Unable to read anything in Wolfe's guarded face, Rowan took refuge in her coffee, drinking it quickly. She covered a yawn as she set down her cup. 'You're right,' she admitted. 'I'm not up to par yet. I'll get you a toothbrush and some toothpaste and do the dishes, then I'll go to bed.'

He ran a reflective hand over his jaw. A strange sensation loosened Rowan's sinews and bones and it felt as though her temperature shot skywards. Perhaps, she thought hopefully, I'm getting a fever rather than making an idiot of myself over him.

'Do you have a spare razor?' he said.

'Disposable ones,' she told him, daring him to ask who they were for. 'I'll put them on the bathroom bench with the toothbrush and toothpaste.'

With automatic courtesy he stood as she got up, but she felt his intent, speculative regard follow her and Lobo through the door.

It took only a moment to leave the necessary toiletries in the bathroom; by the time she came out her defences were slammed back into place and double-locked.

Wolfe was walking silently down the hall towards her. After a searching look he said, 'You look exhausted. Go to bed—I'll deal with the dishes.'

With sudden, unexpected insight she sensed that beneath that iron self-control churned violent, consuming emotions; the knowledge undermined her resistance and desperately excited her.

'Thank you,' she said in a muted voice.

He said abruptly, as though driven to it, 'Rowan, tell me what happened to Tony. Otherwise he'll always be between us.'

Her breath locked in her throat. 'What do you mean?'

Her life was now unbelievably complicated because of the man who stood there looking at her with enigmatic eyes in which all emotions were drowned by the depth of colour. He wasn't promising anything—and she couldn't give him what he wanted, not even with that half-suggestion, that hint that perhaps they might have some sort of future, tempting her with forbidden strength.

Wearily she said, 'There's nothing more I can tell you.'

She expected a flash of anger, perhaps even more threats, but his lashes covered his eyes for a second and when they lifted she saw no more than a glimmering green opacity, burnished and depthless. 'A pity. Goodnight, Rowan.' His voice was toneless, without inflection.

'Yes,' she said, adding with a rush, 'Goodnight.'

Clutching her dignity around her, she hurried through her evening ritual in the bathroom, warily listening to Wolfe's movements in the kitchen. It was a huge relief to firmly close the door of her bedroom.

Eventually she drifted into a light, restless sleep, but when Lobo broke into ferocious barking she woke in stark panic, her eyes staring painfully through the thick

darkness, her skin pulled tight as her heart pounded unevenly in her throat.

Such was her stupor that she had to think before she
identified Wolfe's voice through the din of Lobo's warning.

'What's going on?' she demanded, scrambling out of
bed and racing out into the hall.

Judging by the noise, Lobo was facing the verandah
door. She blinked several times until she could discern
Wolfe's dark silhouette between her and the dog. His
curt command stopped Lobo's truculent defiance of
whatever was outside, but at the sound of Rowan's voice
the dog began again, loud barks that filled the hall and
rang in her ears.

'No!' Rowan commanded, trying to push past the man
who blocked her way.

In one smooth movement Wolfe grabbed her and
yanked her behind the broad shield of his body. 'Stay
there,' he ordered almost soundlessly. 'I heard something outside.'

Lobo subsided into a state of hyper-awareness, growling deep in his throat, his attention fixed on the door
and whatever was beyond it.

Shaken, Rowan responded, 'It could be anything—a
stoat, or a rat running across the verandah. Even a sea-
bird blown in by the wind. Lobo's fiercely territorial.'

'It goes with the name,' Wolfe said almost soundlessly. 'It wasn't an animal.'

Her eyes, adjusting to the darkness, took in the clas-
sical masculine outline in front of her—the wedge of
shoulders and chest narrowing to lean waist and hips—
dimly illuminated by the dying glow of the embers in
the sitting room. Like her, Wolfe hadn't paused to grab
a dressing gown, but, unlike her, he wore no other

clothes. She registered the musky scent of male, clean and potent.

Wildfire sensation rioted along every nerve in her body. Taking a hurried step back, she said huskily, 'He quite often barks at nothing.'

'He's not barking at nothing now. I'll go out and—'

'No!' Prey to so many emotions she couldn't disentangle them, she drew in a ragged breath. 'He's calmed down. Whatever it was has gone.'

When Wolfe didn't move she had a sudden feeling of suffocation, of threat. Swallowing surreptitiously to ease an arid throat, she went on, 'We'll check tomorrow morning.'

The oppressive tension eased slightly. Yet Wolfe still waited with a lethal stillness that had something predatory, almost inhumanly patient about it, and although Lobo was no longer growling, she sensed his alertness.

Rowan said, 'I think we should get back to bed.'

Another gust of wind roared in over the pohutukawas, rattling the windows, keening around the corners. Rowan had half turned when a huge noise engulfed them, groaning, rushing—almost screaming—followed by a thump that came up through the floor.

Lobo went berserk, and Rowan made for the door, only to be brought up short by Wolfe's grip on her arm.

'Stay right there,' he commanded. 'That sounded like a tree. It's too dangerous to go outside.'

'A *tree*?' She noted with irony that Wolfe had been promoted to head of the pack in Lobo's mind—as soon as he spoke, Lobo stopped barking.

In the sudden silence as the wind sank into stillness she said thinly, 'It's probably the old oak. Jim was going to help me cut it down, and—well, Jim's a dear, but fishing comes first.'

Wolfe's grip relaxed, but he didn't release her. 'How close is it to the house? Could any stray branch hit the roof?'

'No,' she said quickly, staving off any suggestion that he go outside and check. Another squall announced its arrival with a howl and a hiss of rain. She finished edgily, 'The branch I was worried about was on the far side. I'm not going outside in that, and there's no need for you to, either.'

Desperate to get away, she turned too abruptly in the darkness. Her head swam, and she put out her hand to find the wall. It met bare skin lightly dusted with hair. She froze, her whole being concentrated in her fingertips, dangerously sensitive to the smooth, taut bulge of muscle and the heat of Wolfe's fine-grained skin.

Get out of here, she ordered herself, but hunger ambushed her, fierce and wild, and she thought despairingly, When he accepts that he can't force me to tell him about Tony he'll go, and this fever and urgency is all I'll have to remember, because in this we're equal—reluctant prisoners...

'Wolfe,' she whispered, all thought submerged in the acute pleasure that rioted through her.

'What?'

But he knew. She'd have stepped back and gone to her bedroom as some dim spark of reason told her she should—right now!—if she hadn't recognised the primal understanding beneath the challenge in his tone.

He was just as affected by the slow glide of her fingertips across his skin as she was; she felt his chest rise and fall when he dragged an ungentle breath into his lungs.

Rowan had craved this moment every second of the past long weeks since they'd made love—an innocent joining, because then neither had known of the tragic link between them.

That innocence was important to her, although she couldn't remember why. Fragments of disconnected thoughts tumbled lazily in her head as she traced his shoulder to the swell of his upper arm.

'Do you work out?' she asked in a drowsy voice.

His low laughter accused her of cowardice. 'Do you care?'

'No,' she said, surrendering to temptation with a long, slow sigh. She held up her face and touched her tongue to his throat, tasting him with a heated abandon that held a touch of shyness. If the light had been on she wouldn't have dared—but here in the friendly darkness she could break free of her fears and forebodings.

'I don't care about anything,' she whispered into his mouth. God help her, at that moment it was the truth.

Wolfe couldn't control the odd sound from his throat, half-purr, half-growl, nor could he withhold the kiss she was angling for.

Even though he knew she was probably trying to distract him with sex, his arms clamped around her slender, fragrant body. The thin cotton of her nightshirt didn't give her any protection at all from his aroused body, but she didn't seem to want any. She swayed into him, yielding to his mouth with a seductive, dangerous ardour that swamped his brain with fumes of drugging sexuality.

When he managed to summon enough determination to break the kiss, Wolfe kissed her throat, and then nipped her earlobe. She responded with a gasping little sound that stoked the fire in him.

No other woman, he thought desperately, trying to clear his head of her sweetly carnal scent, had ever been able to do this to him. Damn it, why couldn't he remember that she was the enemy…?

The words he'd used before echoed in his ears: *Tell me what happened to Tony. Otherwise he'll always be between us…*

He'd almost reached her then; he knew it. She'd looked at him with something like hope, before returning the usual evasive answer. Perhaps this shy, clever come-on was an attempt to follow up his admission that he wanted her.

Did she think she could use sex to persuade him that there were better things to do than finding out who'd killed Tony?

Her skin tasted like honey and wine mixed with a tang that was all her own. In spite of everything, Wolfe admitted with a slow, consuming anger, he still wanted her with a ferocity that hadn't died in the intervening weeks.

Well, two could play at using sex. Lifting his head, he slid a hand over the warm, expectant curve of her breast, moulding it with a sensuous expertise, coldly pleased at her shaken breath and the sudden fluttering down of her lashes.

That first mating had been gentle; as soon as he'd realised she was a virgin an inexplicable pleasure and awe had tempered his strength. Now he wanted her to match him with the same gut-twisting fierceness. He wanted to take her to bed and spend hours stamping his possession on her, making her so much his that she'd never be able to look at another man with that lying desire in her eyes.

With sudden cruelty he kissed her again.

This time she yielded fully, opening her mouth to the erotic exploration of his, exploring in her turn, and Wolfe forgot that he was playing for high stakes.

Some time during that kiss he picked her up and carried her into the nearest bedroom, kicking the door shut in Lobo's face. Slowly he slid her down his aroused body, smiling in the darkness as she flowed over him. His fingers slid her shirt up and over her head while he lowered her onto the bed and followed her down.

Rowan expected it to be like the first time, but Wolfe had other ideas. He didn't speak, but as the rain thundered on the roof he taught her more about her body than she had ever known, taught her that pleasure was a serious concept worthy of the utmost time and effort.

His hands were skilful and sure and gentle as they rediscovered her, yet they trembled when she modelled her caresses on his. She learned to expect the exquisite sensations when his mouth explored her breasts, learned that they were compounded when he kissed the rest of her skin, stoking the fires until she twisted and moaned against him, her hands greedy and demanding as she explored his body, her voice caught in the back of her throat.

And then, when she was moaning his name in an urgent, erotic plea, he said harshly, 'It's not going to work, Rowan. I don't know how far you're prepared to go— but I'm not prepared to risk making you pregnant. And, however often we make love, I'm not going to let you off the hook until I find out how Tony died.'

Crashing down from a sexual high, Rowan froze for a shocked, humiliated moment, before scrabbling off the side of the bed.

He didn't try to keep her there. Instead he lay on his side as she fumbled for her shirt.

'It's probably on the floor somewhere,' he drawled, and turned.

'I've got it,' she said, raw with shame and already halfway to the door.

He laughed, and said an insolent 'Goodnight' as she fled.

Lobo met her outside, but she closed her door against him. Back in her empty room, in her cold bed, shivering with lonely humiliation, she seethed silently as the wind faded and the rain began to ease.

She hated Wolfe Talamantes—*loathed* him!—so how on earth had she fallen in love with him? And when? He'd done nothing but make love to her with bewildering ardour, and threaten her.

OK, so he'd cared for her when she'd fallen into the water, but that wasn't enough to wreak this bewildering, embarrassing change in her emotions.

She had no specific moment to go back to and say, Before that I didn't love him, and now I do. His impact on her had been like lightning, like a thunderclap, so dramatic that she'd thought it nothing more than potent sexual sorcery, fool's gold against the real ore.

But now, when it was too late, she understood the truth. All the time she'd been fencing with him, fascinated, exhilarated and scared, her heart had been betraying her into love. She'd never be the same again.

She woke late to a complete change of weather—a perfect Sunday morning.

After dressing quietly in jeans and a sweatshirt, she and Lobo tiptoed out into a world renewed. Sunlight, thick and golden, shimmered over the bay, turning the view into a picture from a book of fables.

Normally her spirits would have soared. This morning, although she noted the beauty, she gazed at it with empty eyes until she saw the carnage caused by the storm. One of the huge lower branches on the old oak had indeed smashed its way to the ground in a wild tangle of branches, leaving a jagged stump and a great wound in the main trunk.

Her grandfather had told her about his grandfather, the man who'd built the house and settled the land and planted the oak tree in memory of his oldest child, drowned in the bay below.

Tears aching at the back of her throat, she was surveying the tangled mess of branch and leaves when Wolfe said from behind, 'The whole tree is dangerous. It should be felled.'

She swung around, her heart somersaulting in her chest. Lobo, the traitor, merely sat and looked on, tongue lolling after an energetic tussle with a branch.

Wolfe must have already been out to the yacht, because he'd changed from the clothes she'd washed the previous night. Sunlight edged his profile, making his face into an image carved from heroic prehistory— strong and imbued with power. He wasn't looking at the tree; he was watching her with cold speculation.

Bracing herself, Rowan said, 'I know.'

She tried to smile as Lobo dived into the fallen greenery to emerge with a stick in his mouth, which he laid with a flourish at her feet.

Wolfe drawled, 'Now that you know I'm not going to be manipulated through sex, how much will it take for you to tell me exactly what happened the day Tony died?'

Her astounded gaze clashed with eyes deeper and darker than the deepest reaches of the sea, eyes that made green something to drown in. 'What?' she asked numbly.

'I'm talking money.' He was the businessman, cold,

lethal. 'How much do you want to unlock those memories, Rowan?'

She had thought he couldn't humiliate her any further. White-lipped, she asked, 'How much are you prepared to pay?'

Lip curling, he said, 'Enough to set you up for life. My mother is important to me,' and named a sum that made her gasp.

Her hand stole down to Lobo's head. Lifting her head, she fought back bitterness and an aching, hollow anguish to say curtly, 'I don't want your money. For the last time, I can't tell you anything more.' With sudden passion she demanded, 'Will you please get out of here and never, never come back? I don't ever want to see or hear anything about you or your family again.'

In a voice slow and lazy and silken with menace, he said, 'Tough. I'm not going until I get what I want.'

'So how is your huge empire functioning without you?' she snapped back.

He smiled. 'I'm in contact. That's the virtue of computers and modern electronics—there is nowhere in the world anyone can hide. You're going to talk, either to me or my mother, or you'll find you have no future, no career and no peace ever again.'

He meant it, and he had the power to do it. Rowan said sickly, 'So the real Wolfe Talamantes reveals himself at last.'

Lobo leapt to his feet and began to bark, stopping after the first fusillade with the air of a dog who recognises the sound coming towards him. Sure enough, Jim's battered truck appeared around the corner of the drive, and Jim himself grinned at them all as he climbed stiffly out of it.

'Gidday, Rowan, Wolfe.' He stooped to pat Lobo's

eager head, and reached onto the tray for a large plastic sack. 'Rowan, don't you try to fell that tree by yourself. I'll give you a hand.'

'Thank you,' Rowan said, so glad to see him she could have kissed his gnarled, amiable face. Jim was a darling, but the help he offered, although sincerely meant, would never eventuate.

He said, 'Went out yesterday and got a couple of smallish kingies for you. They've been in the chiller, but you'd better cut 'em up as soon as you can.'

Rowan nodded and bent to pick up the sack. She was forestalled by Wolfe, who lifted it with no appreciable effort.

'Thank you,' she said coolly. Driven by the need to keep a distance between her and the man who had just threatened her with the ruin of her life, she asked swiftly, 'Jim, would you like breakfast? A cup of tea?'

'Nah, Kevin and me are off to Furniss Rock to check his craypots. Catch you later.' He climbed into the truck, waved, and headed back down the drive.

Rowan held out her hand for the sack, saying remotely, 'I'll take that.'

'It's too heavy,' Wolfe said, shrewd eyes surveying her with excruciating thoroughness, their faint golden spangles glittering beneath the thick lashes. 'Rowan, just tell me,' he said softly. 'That's all you have to do.'

Rowan tried to control the pulses that sped into overdrive as he smiled at her, a smile exciting enough to set any female heart careering down an unthinking and reckless road.

Before she was overwhelmed by its formidable temptation, the hard-edged, masculine magnetism of it, she counter-attacked with biting scorn. 'Please go, Mr

Talamantes. I don't need anything at all from you—not your money or your help—'

'I'm sure you don't *need* anything,' he interrupted, sounding bored, 'but my parents taught me that it was polite to carry things for women—especially heavy fish. It's a conditioned response. What do you want done with these?'

Pivoting, she strode towards the house, snapping at Lobo to heel when he took too keen an interest in the plastic sack.

'Put them in the tub, please.' She lifted the filleting knife from the block.

'I'll do it.' Wolfe stretched out an imperative hand.

'It's all right. I don't suppose you'll have much experience—'

He said between his teeth, 'I don't know where you got this idea that I'm spoilt, useless and incompetent— or perhaps I do.'

'Tony never said a derogatory word about you,' she flashed back, pleased because she'd managed to break through his cold surface of self-command. 'I knew he had a brother in Hong Kong, that was all.'

'I grew up as a normal human being,' he said with a bite in the words. 'My father and I went fishing. I know how to fillet a fish and how to cut it into steaks.'

Wordlessly, Rowan handed over the knife and the steel. Wolfe sharpened the knife with a swift, almost ferocious dexterity, an efficient amalgam of force and skill that appealed to her at the same time as it intensified her caution into wariness. After watching him for a moment, she sharpened another knife and got to work on the second fish.

To break the taut silence, she asked, 'Have you got something personal against that fish?'

His glance was as edged as the knife. 'No. Whatever I do, I like to do well,' he said pleasantly. 'And I don't give up until it's finished.'

Rowan shivered. Without speaking she finished her smaller fish, took out plastic bags and began to pack the fillets for the freezer.

So he was angry? Good, so was she. Anger kept the bleak desolation at bay.

Wolfe put his knife down. 'What do you do with the leftovers?'

She usually made stock, but she already had enough to keep her going for a while. 'I'll bury them.'

'I'll do it. Where?'

Warned by the note in his voice, she said, 'Under the apple tree by the vegetable garden—through the gap in the guava hedge. The spade's in the shed there. Dig the hole deep enough so that Lobo can't get to the bottom.'

Ever hopeful, the dog frisked off beside Wolfe as Rowan began to stack the bags of fish into the freezer. When she'd finished she scrubbed her hands and went out.

Wolfe was shovelling the earth back into the hole, the smooth, rhythmic movements of his arms and shoulders personifying power and co-ordination. A safe distance away, Lobo watched, head tilted on one side.

Anguish tore through Rowan, almost bringing her to her knees. Before she had a chance to straighten up, strong hands caught her and dragged her upright.

'Are you all right?' The words were a soft growl in the back of Wolfe's throat. 'What happened?'

'I tripped,' she lied. 'It's getting to be a habit. I'm fine.'

He released her and stood back, leaving her to deal

with the after-effects of lightning, a cold and dangerous electricity rampaging through her cells.

'Watch where you're going,' he said, his smile and tone blending so that the words seemed an ancient incantation, a charm to burn away inhibitions and produce instant and complete surrender.

Oh, God, she thought despairingly, clenching her teeth against the urge to fling herself back into his arms.

Making love with him had released a hidden, devouring need, a hunger that stripped away her self-esteem by revealing how shallow and feeble she really was, unable to resist a marauder who'd deliberately humiliated her.

She didn't know—she didn't *want* to know—the Rowan Corbett who could sink fathoms deep into the open carnality of sex with an aggressive, antagonistic stranger.

But then, even at their first meeting he hadn't been a stranger to her.

'Stop looking at me like that,' he rasped.

Pulses jumping, her breath coming shallow and fast, she tried to drag her gaze away from his hard face. He said something she didn't hear, and then reached for her, crushing her into his arms. But he didn't kiss her, and she could feel the taut, lethal stillness in his big body as he fought for control.

With Wolfe's arms around her and her cheek pressed into his throat, she began to dimly comprehend how a primitive part of the brain could neutralise logic and reason. He smelt of musk, she thought, fascinated by the shuddering beat of his heart.

Mixed in with this faint, evocative scent was the clean tang of the sea. If she licked him he'd probably taste of salt.

At this thought something inside her deliquesced, imploded. Greedily desiring a satisfaction she'd never know again, she had to stifle a crazy urge to delicately, slowly, run the tip of her tongue across the strong, warm column of his throat so that she could taste as well as inhale the other component that made up his individual scent, the indefinable essence of Wolfe Talamantes— barely noticeable and yet more potently male than the musk and the salt together.

'Rowan.'

The contempt in his voice shocked her into awareness. Bitterly ashamed of the weakness that had kept her motionless, she wrenched herself free.

He let her go, surveying her hot face with merciless eyes. 'However enthusiastically you fling yourself at me, I'm not going to stop asking you what happened when Tony died,' he said with freezing clarity.

The wild colour drained from her skin as she seized on anger with an eagerness that owed everything to humiliation. 'I never for a moment thought you would,' she snarled.

His eyes flicked down at her breasts. She knew what he saw there—her nipples shamelessly erect against the material.

Wolfe's smile didn't reach the depthless eyes. 'So it won't work,' he advised.

She shrugged. 'Worth a try,' she said laconically, ignoring the glitter in his dark eyes to say, 'I've wrapped some fish for you. I assume you have a chiller on your opulent boat.'

'All the mod cons,' he returned coolly. 'If that's a heavy hint that you want to see the back of me, all you had to do was say so.'

She stiffened at the smooth challenge in his tone, but

didn't take him up on it. 'I'm sure you have things to do, places to go.'

'Things to do, anyway.' He shouldered the spade and walked back to the woodshed with it. 'I don't plan to go anywhere in the immediate future.'

Five minutes later, fish in hand, he disappeared under the branches of the pohutukawa trees. As Lobo whined, Rowan turned away and said wretchedly, 'We'd better have a talk about loyalty, I think. However, that can wait until I've done some serious, money-earning work.'

But she lingered in the shelter of the pohutukawas, waiting to see Wolfe climb onto his yacht before she turned away and went into the studio. Once before, when her world had crashed around her, she'd found comfort and a kind of redemption in work. 'I can do it again,' she told Lobo, who curled up and went to sleep in a patch of sun.

Except that she couldn't settle, didn't even turn on the wheel.

Instead, she picked up a pencil and began to doodle, realising some minutes later that she was sketching Wolfe's face. Squinting, she tried to remember the exact proportions of eyes to nose to jaw, the way the light and shade fell across it, subtly delineating the muscles and bone structure beneath. But, although she had some small skill in drawing, she couldn't get him right.

Eventually she sat with her eyes closed and lingered over the strong contours in her mind, deliberately imprinting them so that when she was old she'd be able to summon his face just by closing her eyes.

Her fingers flew across the paper as she committed him to it.

A short sharp bark from Lobo got her to her feet. 'Jim—oh, *no*.'

It was Wolfe, in fresh clothes, and something about the way he walked, the hardness of his face, chilled her.

She met him at the workshop door. 'What is it?'

'My mother's in hospital,' he told her with icy precision. 'They think she's going to die, and this time, Rowan, you have no choice. Get some clothes packed and organise Lobo's board for a couple of days. Or we can take him with us. There's a helicopter on its way.'

'I'm so sorry,' she said with swift sympathy, and then realised what he'd said. 'Wolfe, I can't tell her what happened,' she said painfully. 'I *can't*...'

For a split second she saw rage, deep and murderous, in his face. Instantly he controlled it, but not before she'd taken a shaken step backwards.

In a voice that slashed through her fragile composure he said, 'You're going to Auckland if I have to tie and gag you. And once there you'll tell her what happened that day, or you can contemplate what your life will be like once I've finished with you. My mother is more important to me than you will ever be.'

'You can't kidnap me,' she said feverishly.

'Watch me.' His glance was hard, sword-edged. 'The only other choice you've got is to tell *me* exactly what happened to Tony.'

He meant it; the threat was overt, unmasked, and he looked capable of shaking the truth out of her. She could set Lobo on him—no, of course she couldn't. She understood his pain; she'd have sacrificed Tony for her father.

Only she hadn't been given the choice.

Wolfe's voice softened a fraction as he added, 'If you feel that you have to protect someone, I meant what I said before—I'm interested in the truth, not in blaming anyone.'

She looked up sharply. He met her eyes with a straight level gaze that reassured some deep-seated instinct. 'Can I trust you?' she asked desperately.

'Yes.'

Simply said, but he meant that too. Cravenly Rowan realised that by telling him she'd hand the responsibility over to him. He could decide what to say to his mother.

Turning back into the workshop, she said tiredly, 'All right, I'll tell you.'

CHAPTER NINE

ROWAN walked across to the potting wheel. Head bent, she said, 'When I met Tony at Cooksville I really liked him, but…'

'But what?' Wolfe demanded.

Rowan spread out her hands in a swift negative gesture. 'Before long I—he became too…'

'Too what?' When she didn't answer he insisted lethally, 'Tell me, damn you.'

'Too intense,' she muttered, unable to think of a better word.

'Tony? Intense?' His voice was cold and scathing. 'You'll have to do better than that, Rowan. Tony was the light-hearted one, bright and happy and always entertaining. I doubt if he ever had an intense thought in his life—even after his accident he joked his way through convalescence.'

'That was how he seemed at first,' she said wearily, looking around at her work, at the room so familiar yet now forever different because Wolfe was standing in it. 'When I went to Auckland he changed.'

'Changed?'

She wriggled her shoulders, trying to ease the tension knotting them. 'He seemed to think he had rights—rights I wasn't prepared to concede.'

'What rights?'

'Rights to my life! He wanted to know where I was all the time, what I was doing, who I was with. At first I was flattered, but I started to resent the way he tried to make me report to him. He wouldn't accept that what I was doing was really important to me. He'd ring up and suggest a day out on the harbour, a trip to Queenstown, a weekend in Australia, and when I said I had to work he'd be angry and dismissive. After a couple of months it got too much, so I told him I thought it was time to cool things for a while.'

Wolfe's mouth compressed. 'If you were lukewarm enough to dump him because he wanted to be with you, why did you follow him to Auckland?'

'I did *not* follow him to Auckland,' she snapped, goaded into rash anger. 'I've already told you this. Why don't you believe me?'

'Because Tony said otherwise.'

Rowan swung around and confronted him, eyes like golden fire in a white, determined face. 'And Tony never lied?'

'Not to me,' he said levelly.

She closed her eyes a second, opening them to say steadily, 'He was always very plausible, and I suppose you had a vested interest in believing him.' She didn't know whether Wolfe believed her or not, and as she ploughed on she told herself she didn't care. 'A man with your contacts could certainly verify that I'd been accepted by the School of Arts well before I met Tony.'

Judging by Wolfe's cold green scrutiny, he didn't believe a word of it. Well, he wanted the truth—now he was going to get it!

Recklessly she added, 'I wanted a lot more from life than to play with a spoiled brat.'

Still in the same uncompromising tone, Wolfe said, 'Yes, he was spoiled. But he certainly wasn't lacking in female company—why would he fixate on you?'

'I don't know, but when I refused to go out with him

he started stalking me,' she said starkly, the little pulse in her throat hammering as she remembered the fear that had gradually overshadowed her life.

'Stalking you?' Wolfe's comment, and the look that came with it, was little short of contemptuous. 'You hinted that before. I don't believe it.'

Rowan walked across to the window and pushed it wide open. Dragging in a breath of fresh, warm air, she said unevenly, 'I don't know what else to call it. He rang the hostel night and morning, asking for me. He always seemed to know where I was going, what I was doing. If I went out at night he'd be there waiting, or he'd soon turn up. He sent flowers and gifts—which I sent back—and wrote letters. Hundreds of letters.' Something in Wolfe's face made her stop.

'Do you have any of them?' he demanded.

She shivered. 'No, I burnt them.'

'So there's no evidence. You're going to have to do better than this,' Wolfe said scornfully. 'You said Tony was spoiled—he certainly was for choice when it came to women. He wouldn't have dreamed of investing so much time and effort in one who turned him down.'

The last colour drained from her face. 'Why would I lie? If you don't believe me, I'll give you the names of my friends, the ones I confided in.'

'Who presumably would lie for you,' he said implacably.

It was like hitting a stone wall. 'They thought I was mad to be so uptight,' she said, forcing the words out. 'They called him the last of the red-hot romantics. Even my father felt I was making a mountain out of a mole-hill.' She stopped, skin clammy as she recalled her growing fear, her frightening inability to do anything about Tony's steady, patient, remorseless pursuit.

Wolfe frowned. 'Go on.'

His ruthless insistence forced her to admit, 'He never said anything that could be taken as a threat, but he was trying to take over my life, herd me into a place where he set the boundaries and made the decisions.' She watched her forefinger drawing a pattern in the dried film of clay—slashing downward bars. In a shaking voice she went on, 'I know it sounds melodramatic, but I felt that he wanted to coop me up in his own personal prison. He made my life a misery. He took photos of me with a telephoto lens, then posted them to me—without the negatives. I felt as though I was being watched all the time, even in the bathroom.'

Acutely aware of Wolfe's deepening frown, she turned back to the window and breathed deeply again, staring at the wreck of the tree on the lawn. Dark sap oozed slowly from the jagged end of the broken branch. 'On my twenty-first birthday he talked a couple of my friends into staging a party, and I had to pretend to enjoy it. He was on a high...'

That was when she'd felt real fear, because Tony's gloating smile and the glitter in his eyes had promised something even worse. Aloud she said unevenly, 'Half-way through the evening, in front of them all, he produced a ring and went down on one knee and proposed.' She stopped, her hand going to her throat as she relived the suffocating feeling of being trapped. Beads of cold sweat began to gather at her temples.

'What did you do?' Wolfe's voice was unyielding.

From some reservoir of strength she found her voice. 'I tried to laugh it off, but when he grabbed my hand and began to force the ring on my finger, I said no.'

'What happened?' Wolfe asked inflexibly.

She sent him a swift glance, meeting cold eyes as

polished as enamel. 'He made it all into a huge joke, but underneath he was furious. When everyone had gone, we had a horrible, huge row. In the end, he—he cried, and begged me not to leave him and promised me...' Her voice trailed away.

'Money,' Wolfe supplied harshly.

'Yes.' She looked down at the finger which Tony had gripped painfully while he'd tried to force a huge diamond ring onto it. In a muted voice she went on, 'He wouldn't listen—he was like a man possessed. He terrified me.'

'Why? Because your chickens had come home to roost?'

Nonplussed, she stared at him. 'What do you mean?'

'I mean,' Wolfe said sardonically, 'that, having tormented him into the kind of humiliation no man could stand, you got scared when he lost control. Surely your father warned you about teasing men, and told you that sooner or later one of them would snap?'

Fists clenching at her sides, Rowan took a step towards him, so angry she could barely articulate the words that frothed up inside her.

But why blame him? Even her father had fallen for Tony's facile charm, and he hadn't had Wolfe's natural affection for his younger brother. Tony had won again.

Grey hopelessness drowning her anger, she said, 'I realise you're finding this difficult to believe—'

'Difficult? Actually, I'm admiring your creativity.'

Rowan had had enough. This morning, with the cold calculation of a cash register, this man had offered her money too—huge amounts of it, enough to buy her a future—after he'd made love to her and then rejected her. Why on earth was she trying to make this easier for him?

She said with savage clarity, 'Obviously you have no idea—and don't have the imagination or desire to understand—just how terrifying it is to have someone try to take over your life, force you to fit into their mould, be what they want, do what they tell you. I hope you never discover it.'

He gave her a long, intent look. She met it fearlessly.

'Did you go to the police?' he asked, giving nothing away.

'My father was a cop! He brought me up from birth, and no one could have been more protective, but even he thought I was overreacting. If I couldn't convince him, what hope did I have of making anyone else listen to me? Besides—' She stopped.

'Besides?'

With difficulty she said, 'I wondered whether I was in some way to blame.'

To her surprise Wolfe didn't take her up on that. She glanced across, saw a face sculpted from stone. If only she could make him understand—but how could she expect to? He'd probably never come up against a situation he couldn't master, and it was his half-brother they were talking about. Outside on the lawn a blackbird watched a tuft of grass, head cocked on one side, before snatching a worm from the ground and flying into the flame tree.

Knowing it was futile, Rowan went on, 'I had no way of dealing with him except to be blunt. I told him I didn't love him and I was never going to marry him—that I wasn't going to marry anyone for years yet because I wanted to do something with whatever talent I'd been given.' He'd seized on that, switching in a moment from pleading to laughing scorn. 'He said that I was fooling myself, that my friends sniggered behind my back at me because everyone knew I had no talent.'

She looked past Wolfe to the jaggedly broken branches outside. In a controlled voice she went on, 'Eventually he left, but while I was at class the next day he stole my portfolio from my room at the hostel. He rang me and told me that I could have it back if I moved in with him. One page for each night in his bed. Otherwise he'd burn it.'

Wolfe hadn't moved, and she could read nothing in the disciplined angles and planes of his face. Her voice trembled as she said, 'He knew I needed that portfolio for my final assessment. I threatened him with the police if he didn't return it. He just laughed.'

Tony's laughter—assured, easy—had enraged and frightened her in equal measure. 'So I told him I wouldn't prostitute myself for a portfolio—anything I'd done there I could do again.'

A muscle flicked in Wolfe's jaw. Yes, now he knew how his offer of money had made her feel—like a woman who could be bought. It should have given her some satisfaction, but all she could feel was a vast emptiness, a cry of outrage echoing through her. She fell silent, imprisoned by memories of the lonely horror of those months under siege when she'd been unable to convince anyone of what she was enduring, but she said bleakly, 'Ask your mother. She sent me the portfolio after—after he died. It was in his apartment.'

'And?' Wolfe asked, so harshly that Lobo leapt to his feet and paced across to stand beside her, hackles lifting.

'He said I'd never get away from him—that wherever I went he'd follow me until I realised that I belonged to him. I tried to reason with him, but he didn't care about the real me—I was just a moving, breathing statue he had to possess. He was calm, completely confident. He *knew* what he was doing, and he didn't care.' Cold sweat gathered across her forehead, trickled between her breasts and down her spine. 'That was when I realised I'd never be free of him. I couldn't see how he could do this to me, make my life a complete and utter misery and get away with it, but he was doing it, and there didn't seem to be any way I could stop him.'

She paused before saying in a hoarse voice, 'I ran home for the weekend to sort out what to do next. I had this crazy scheme of hiding in Japan—but I needed to make sure that Dad wouldn't tell him where I was, because Tony had the money to follow me anywhere I went.'

Wolfe's eyes narrowed into piercing green slivers. 'Go on,' he said almost soundlessly.

She wet her lips. 'I went out one Saturday afternoon with a friend, and Tony turned up at the house just as Dad was going to the shooting range. Dad did pistol shooting competitively. Tony went with him, and from what Dad said afterwards they had what he thought was a really constructive chat about the situation.' Her mouth widened in a humourless smile. 'Tony confessed that he'd probably been too pushy, and he told Dad that he was going to pull back and wait until I was ready. He asked my father if he could have some time alone with me, and Dad couldn't see any harm in it. I'd just got home when they came in.'

She swallowed, remembering again the sick panic that had engulfed her at Tony's grin as he'd followed her father into the house—a grin that had turned into vaunting triumph when her father had made an excuse and left the room.

Wolfe watched her with opaque, unreadable eyes. 'What happened?'

'Fear and anger make a pretty powerful mixture. I lost

it,' she said wearily. 'I ordered him out, told him once and for all that I wanted nothing more to do with him, that he was sick and getting sicker, and that no one had the right to do what he'd been doing to me.'

'And how did he respond to that?' Wolfe asked without expression.

Rowan realised she was wringing her hands. Hiding them behind her back, she said in a muffled voice, 'He laughed, as though it was the best joke in the world, then he said I should be grateful he loved me, and that this was one battle I wasn't going to win.'

'And what happened then?'

She closed her eyes and took a shallow, impeded breath, steadying her voice by sheer force of will. 'He'd carried the pistols in and put them on the bench by the door, but he'd been fiddling with them, just casually, the way you do when your mind's not on what you're doing, when you're just occupying your hands.' She stopped and swallowed. 'I saw him doing it, but I was so angry and upset it didn't register. Until—until he lifted a pistol and pointed it at me. I saw Dad come through the door behind him at the moment Tony said quite casually that—that if I didn't agree to marry him he'd kill me, and then himself.'

Abruptly, moving with less of his usual litheness, Wolfe walked across to the window. 'What happened?' he asked harshly, without turning.

'He meant it,' she said tonelessly. 'He said that I had to make the decision then. I—I told him that he didn't need to go so far, but he gave me a sort of glazed stare and said that since his accident he'd realised that he was an all-or-nothing man. If he couldn't have me, no one else was going to.'

When Wolfe cursed beneath his breath she flinched.

He said savagely, 'For God's sake tell me what happened!'

'I talked to him, trying to calm him down. Dad always said that's what you should try to do, and although I didn't dare look at him tiptoeing in, I could feel him willing me to stay calm until he got to Tony, so I kept babbling, trying to cover any noise Dad might make.'

In a cold voice Wolfe said, 'What happened then?'

'Tony listened, but he was smiling as though he'd already won. Dad was halfway across the room when Tony must have sensed he was there. He—he turned around, and then whipped back again.' Her voice broke and she had to stop and drag in several deep breaths. Without looking at Wolfe she went on tonelessly, 'The moment Tony moved Dad shouted at me to drop and I did, rolling myself up into a ball on the floor. I didn't see what happened next, but the pistol went off.'

At last Wolfe's head turned. Stone-faced, merciless, he commanded, 'Finish it.'

She tightened her trembling mouth. 'The bullet went right through Tony's heart and he—he died.'

Shuddering, she closed her eyes against the remembered horror, but when the vivid images froze against her eyelids she opened them again.

Unmoving, silent, Wolfe loomed against the light outside. What else did he want? she wondered half hysterically.

The truth.

She dragged more air into her lungs. Still in the same blank voice she went on, 'And then my father had a heart attack. I called the ambulance and the police, but—it was too late for Tony.'

'So why did you keep quiet about all this?'

Rowan wet her dry lips. 'Because Dad killed Tony.'

'What?' Wolfe stared at her. 'Killed him? How?'

She wiped the sweat from her forehead. 'While they were grappling he forced the gun around and tightened his hand over Tony's on the trigger.'

'And your father told you this?' Wolfe asked incredulously. 'Why?'

'He—he thought I was my mother.' Tears stung the backs of her eyes, clogged her throat. 'He was dying, and he talked to her, explaining what he'd done.'

'Why?' Wolfe's single word was like the crack of a whip.

'Because he realised that Tony meant it—that I'd never be safe. He knew even before the coronary that he was dying, you see—cancer. He hadn't told me, and I'm glad he died from a heart attack—he'd have preferred a swift death.' She wiped the tears from her eyes with the back of her hand. 'But before that he—he coached me about what to say about Tony's death, and said it would be all right, not to worry.' The tears spilled over. 'And he asked me to forgive him for not believing me.'

'So why didn't you tell me this when I asked you first?' Wolfe asked grimly. 'Who were you protecting? The cop who took your father's statement before he died? Did he coach you too? Or just look the other way?'

'Why should I have told you? How will knowing what happened help your mother?' she evaded bitterly. 'I got what I wanted—I was free. But the price of my freedom was two lives. Can you blame me for not wanting anything to do with you and your family?'

She stopped for a few tense seconds, then finished with anguished despair, 'If your mother dies, that's three people Tony will have killed.'

There was a long moment of silence.

Wolfe said, 'My mother felt all along that you were hiding something.' He paused before continuing in a cool, deliberate tone that successfully hid any emotion, 'You've no reason to like us, have you? Tony terrorised you, my mother publicly blamed you, and I threatened you.'

He believed her! A sudden, intense relief shook Rowan back into life. 'I understood why,' she said swiftly. 'You love your mother—of course you wanted to help her. But I couldn't—I don't know whether Dad's superior officer guessed what had happened, but he certainly made it easy for me at the inquest. He doesn't deserve to lose his job because he looked the other way for a man he knew was dying. Wolfe, I had to protect him. Besides, I knew that the truth wouldn't help your mother.'

With flaying self-contempt he answered, 'You're too compassionate. Was that enough reason to harass you, just like Tony? And I didn't have the decency or the self-control to keep my hands off you.'

Rowan shivered. A barely formed hope had just been killed by his words and now lay shattered in her heart. 'I always knew you weren't like Tony,' she said in a flat voice, aware that it was true.

Coldly, quietly, Wolfe went on, 'As a child he had tantrums when he couldn't get his own way. And he was spoilt—he was his father's only child, and his father was determined that no one should break his spirit. He grew out of any open display of anger, but we all knew that he had a violent temper.' He struck a bench with his closed fist. 'I was proud of the way he'd learned to control it. And proud of his persistence in getting what he wanted, even though his manipulative nature concerned

me. But after the accident he changed. We put it down
to his head injuries.'

The skin on Rowan's body tightened unbearably.
She'd made love to this man, been so angry with him
she could barely speak, feared him, been fascinated by
his brilliant mind. Until then, she hadn't been sorry for
him. Quickly, meaninglessly, she told him, 'It probably
was. I know head trauma can alter people's characters.
Wolfe, it wasn't your fault.'

As though he hadn't heard her, he said, 'I think my
mother must have some inkling of his pursuit of you.
Possibly her need to find out what happened is to reassure herself that he didn't hound you to something violent.'

Rowan bit her lip. 'It wasn't her fault, either! What
are you going to tell her?'

'The truth,' he said, implacable and uncompromising.

Rowan opened her mouth to protest, met unsparing
eyes and closed it again. He knew his mother better than
she did.

Something niggling at the back of her mind pushed
forward and she said through the wave of exhaustion
breaking over her, 'How did you find out where I live?'

'A friend of my mother's—the one who came to the
inquest with her—saw you in the café, and told my
mother.' He watched her with pitiless eyes. 'She told me
a few days before we met.'

'Before we—' Rowan's heart stopped in her throat.

'Yes.'

It hurt to breathe. 'So you knew who I was when—?'

'When we made love. Yes.' He was watching her with
aloof calculation, as though none of this was at all important to him.

Rowan's fists knotted at her sides. Pain and anger exploded through her, swamping everything in a rage of betrayal. 'Get out,' she said in a soft voice that had Lobo on his feet and growling. 'Get out and never, *ever* try to see me again.'

Wolfe said, austerely remote, 'I'm sorry for everything I and my family have put you through, especially for bringing back memories you'd probably hoped never to revisit. I'll leave you to the solitude I interrupted. Goodbye, Rowan.' He held out a hand.

Made witless by shock and pain, working on automatic pilot, she stretched out hers. He lifted it and kissed her fingers, and released it, saying with no warmth in his voice, 'Good luck. No doubt I'll be seeing your name in the newspapers often. You have a great talent—keep refining it. And if there's anything I can ever do for you, you have only to ask me.'

It was that final formal offer that froze her into silence. With Lobo pressed against her legs she watched him go, her whole being stormed by unbearable humiliation, the mark of his kiss branded into her skin.

Into her heart.

Numb and speechless, she stayed in the workroom when the helicopter landed on the beach to take him off, stayed there as a couple of men took out the dinghy and navigated the *Circe* out of the little harbour.

Only then, when the colours of sunset stained the sky scarlet and gold, did Rowan walk from the workroom to her house. The first thing she saw there was her father's dressing gown, hanging on the doorknob of the spare bedroom. She picked it up with shaking hands and lifted it to her face, at last giving way to great sobs that tore her heart into tatters.

CHAPTER TEN

'ROWAN, why do you want to wear that same shirt?' Bobo asked, frowning. 'I mean, I'm perfectly happy to lend it to you again, and it does look wonderful on you, but now you must be able to afford…' Her voice trailed away.

Rowan gave her weak smile. 'Humour me,' she said. 'It's a sort of good luck charm.'

Her agent's frown cleared. 'Oh, because everything sold last time? You superstitious thing, you! Take it—it's yours. It looks better on you than it ever did on me,' she added generously. 'Not that you need good luck—what sells your stuff is your creative instinct and your technical brilliance and that other intangible and mysterious quality that only the best artists have. Do you want the *bustier* as well?'

'No, thank you, I've bought a camisole,' Rowan said with a smile that hid, she hoped, her apprehension.

'I must say,' Bobo chattered on, 'I really wondered whether you'd made the right decision, branching out into bronze figurines, but they are magnificent.'

For six months Rowan had worked long, exhausting hours, pouring her heart and her skill into this new medium, and the solo exhibition she'd mounted was a multi-media one, part-sculpture, part-pottery.

'But it's a gamble that's more than paid off,' Bobo said, squinting at herself in the mirror. 'And of course there's the prestige thing. Although you've earned huge kudos for the pottery, somehow people take metal more seriously. Darling old Frank's going to rave in the newspaper again.'

'How do you know? He might hate them.'

'He's already told me he thinks they're wonderful,' Bobo told her happily, waving her mascara wand. Pulling the standard face, she carefully applied a layer to her lashes. 'He was ecstatic at the preview, and he's massively respected, which is great for those of the populace who like to be told what to buy. As well, of course, he really does know what he's talking about.'

Rowan, who cared for only one person's impressions of the showing, nodded and slid the gold and black shirt over her new, expensive black silk camisole, tucking both into the slim black skirt.

Would Wolfe come? She knew he'd been sent an invitation—the gallery owner had added him to his list after the last showing. Butterflies—no, *bats*—had been picketing her stomach for days.

Defiantly she reminded herself that if Wolfe didn't come she'd know it was definitely over, so she could carry on rebuilding her life without him. During the past six months she'd realised that, like her father, she'd only ever love once, but that didn't mean she'd wither away.

At the moment her work seemed a dreary substitute for the man, but eventually this aching, empty heart must heal.

Surely…?

Since that last scene she hadn't seen Wolfe, hadn't heard from him. She'd told him she hadn't wanted anything more to do with his family, and, unlike Tony, he'd taken her at her word.

As months passed her anger and humiliation had faded as she'd accepted that, like her, loyalty had driven him to sacrifice his own advantage for a deeply loved parent.

He'd lied; so had she.

Loneliness had bitten deeper, hardening into passionate regret when she'd remembered the way he'd cared for her, her relish in his keen, incisive intelligence, the potent sexuality that had enthralled her, until eventually she'd found herself wishing he'd ignored her bitter rejection.

Each day she'd bought a newspaper, at first so that she could search for his mother's name in the death notices. When it didn't appear she'd hoped Laura Simpson had found some sort of peace and renewal—and still kept buying, addicted to the articles about Wolfe Talamantes that appeared regularly.

He certainly wasn't eating his heart out for her; he was busy taking the world by storm.

Struggling to lose herself in the supple promise and defiance of clay and the more complicated lure of bronze, she'd tried to reassemble the shattered shards of her life into something sturdy and worthwhile, forcing herself to begin building a circle of acquaintances. Approaching the sculptor who'd lent her his equipment and helped her with the technical aspects of converting her clay models into bronze had been the first step, but not the last.

Yet although burying herself in work had helped her get through the long, dreary months, Wolfe had taken up residence in that precious sanctuary too—whatever she did, wherever she was, he stayed with her.

She still dreamed of green eyes flecked with gold, of a man who bestrode the night like a dark angel. In her sleep she heard Wolfe's voice and felt his hands on her skin, and each morning she woke longing for a love that

would never be hers, a love she channelled into the clay
models she'd converted to bronze.

For the rest—well, she functioned. Wolfe had eased
her demons when he'd believed her; ironic that she'd
learned to love him before he'd learned to trust her.

A few days after his departure she'd received a letter
from his mother.

*I'm so sorry. Wolfe has told me everything, and I can
only ask you to forgive us for hounding you so un-
mercifully. Although there is no excuse for what Tony
did, please believe me when I say that until the accident there was no sign of such deviance in him.
Knowing the truth has reconciled me to his death. I
know you have lost enough through his behaviour to
make his name—our names—a horror to you, but
Wolfe tells me that you have a compassionate heart
and so I hope in time that you can even manage to
think kindly of us—perhaps even of Tony, who caused
you so much pain and fear.*

She'd wished Rowan every good fortune, and said she
was hers, Laura Simpson.

So Wolfe had said she had a compassionate heart. The
compliment meant so much it frightened her, because
eventually he'd put her out of his mind. Lust was a
chancy thing—ignore it for long enough and it died.

But love was a different kettle of fish.

Work was no longer the sole focus of her life, but she
struggled stubbornly on because surrendering to grief
would at last give Tony the power his damaged brain
had so craved.

Summer had arrived with a fanfare of trumpets, blue
and gold and green, alive with the harsh, shrill music of

cicadas and the night calls of kiwi and moreporks, the day lyrics of tui and little grey warblers.

Rowan had picked new dwarf beans while pohutu-kawa flowers dropped in crimson carpets around the trees, clothing the water with colour that slowly drifted away on the tide. When an occasional yacht anchored in the bay she had despised herself for the wild hope that saw her sprinting across the room to pick up binoculars with shaky hands—and for her intense disappointment when not one was *Circe*.

Now, in Bobo's flat, she was dressing for another exhibition. Would Wolfe come?

Get real.

Why should he? she thought, applying the cosmetics she'd bought that day with a careful but unpractised hand while the bats in her stomach whirled and flew and waved their picket cards, and taut anticipation warred with common sense. He was probably on the other side of the world, swashbuckling another million dollars into his bank account.

She looked with over-bright eyes at a trembling mouth and brilliant cheeks that owed nothing to cosmetics.

'You look—great,' Bobo said, after another keen glance. 'Right, let's go.'

People crowded into the gallery, talking, laughing, eyeing each other, quite a few even looking at the exhibits.

'Everyone's here,' Bobo told her gleefully. 'And lots are buying.'

Rowan cradled a glass of champagne, trying not to look too obviously for a black head above the crush.

'Everyone who's anyone's here!' Georgie confided later, sleek and satisfied and beaming. 'Have to say, Rowan, I wondered if you knew what you were doing when Bobo said you were sculpting, but by God you've made a real breakthrough. They love them! And so they should.'

Rowan kept looking, but as the evening wore on she had to accept that Wolfe wasn't going to arrive.

She thought she'd prepared herself for it, but cold, bone-deep pain ached through every cell in her body. It made no difference that she was mourning a love she'd never had, that she and Wolfe had shared no more than a violent, wholly sexual passion.

'Rowan?' Bobo's voice from behind, but oddly uncertain.

Rowan summoned a smile and turned. 'Yes?'

And froze as she met greenstone eyes in a face carved from granite. A pulse of joy so intense she almost staggered surged through her. The strength and urgency of her emotions shivered across her skin, screwing her nerves to an unbearable pitch.

'You already know Wolfe,' Bobo said in a rush as she looked from one to the other. 'I'll get you something to drink,' she told him, and slid away into the crowd like a rabbit confronted by a wolfhound.

Rowan didn't see her go. Her first incandescent relief was flickering, fading with the renewed beating of her heart. 'What are you doing here?' she asked, barely above a whisper, but he heard her.

'I recognised the scar,' he said, flicking open the catalogue to show her the photograph.

A male torso she'd called *Love*. And there, just below the shoulder, was the scar she'd never seen, the one she'd only ever touched when they made love.

Her eyes searched his face, meeting nothing but unyielding determination in his eyes, in his features, in the ruthless line of his mouth.

'I never found out how you got it,' she said, wondering whether he was angry with her blatant declaration, or had decided that the kindest thing to do was ignore it.

But if so, why had he come? Fickle hope soared again, lending a fugitive colour to her cheekbones.

'You never asked.' His voice was level, without inflection. 'Tony did it. When he was about ten I caught him playing with my Swiss Army knife, something he was strictly forbidden to do. He'd already cut himself on it twice, but of course he desperately wanted one. I told him off and he got angry and threw it at me just as I turned my back on him.'

She drew in an appalled breath. Wolfe shrugged. 'He was terrified when it hit me, and ran away.'

'Wolfe!' a female voice cried with the sort of enthusiasm that proclaimed a long and fascinating history together.

He nodded at the woman, a redhead Rowan dimly recognised, grasped Rowan's elbow and said, 'Sorry, Tessa, but we're just leaving.'

Still a prisoner of that wild uprising of joy, Rowan went with him as far as the door, but there she suddenly dug her heels in. 'No, wait—'

'Come on,' he said curtly. 'Let's get out of here.'

'Bobo—'

But Bobo was waving from the edge of the crowd, her small face alight with mischief. Nevertheless, Wolfe's hand dropped.

With stiff politeness he said, 'I'm sorry. I need to talk to you, but if you want to stay here, we'll stay.'

After a swift glance at his expressionless face she returned abruptly, 'I'll—we might as well go,' and set off again. He didn't touch her again, and at the street door she said, 'I didn't think you were coming.'

'You had to make the first move,' he told her, austerely inflexible. 'Tony had damaged you enough. I had to show you I wasn't like him.'

And that was when she accepted with her brain as well as her instinct and emotions that he spoke the truth.

Both were silent until he'd parked in the basement of the huge apartment block and they'd taken the private lift up to the penthouse. Halfway there Rowan asked thinly, 'How is your mother?'

Wolfe's shoulders, made even broader by the black jacket and white shirt, lifted. 'Her doctor isn't talking miracles, but it seems like one to me,' he said drily. 'She's much better.'

'I'm glad.' She couldn't think of anything else to say.

And once inside the apartment any coherent thought vanished from her mind. Eyes glittering, Wolfe closed the door behind them and turned her gently to face him, saying roughly, 'I've been waiting for this since the day I left you.'

Taut and expectant, Rowan nodded. If sex was all they had, well, she'd accept that. For the present anyway, she thought vaguely, looking into his eyes and floating through clouds of fireflies, of golden sparks glittering in volcanic green air—air the colour of thunderstorms...

She was drawn to him like a moth summoned by the flame, a phoenix following a preordained path to the fire that would kill it and renew it.

Grimly he said, 'We should talk first.'

But Rowan went into the arms that awaited her, saying his name, the name written in letters of dark fire and ecstasy and danger across her mind. 'Later. We can do that later.'

Honey sweetness filled her mouth, heat licked across her skin, and sensation drenched her with delight—warm and heavy and indolent, fresh with promise.

'Rowan,' Wolfe said softly. 'Don't tempt me too far. What I have to tell you is important.'

More important than this? She lifted weighted lids. Behind his stark features she sensed a starving need that called to her with a powerful, sorcerer's voice.

She smiled.

It was the smile that smashed through Wolfe's self-control like bullets through tissue paper. He knew they should get the talking over first—he knew that taking her with the finesse of a stag in rut must kill something in their relationship—but her smile answered a need that had eaten away his will power, a hunger he'd never recognised until he'd met her.

Like the first ever summer, like the promise of paradise, her red mouth beckoned with lazy, untamed desire. Between thick, black lashes the topaz glow of each iris was being swallowed by the dilating pupils.

In artless, almost innocent sensuality she turned her lovely face and nuzzled his throat.

She'd taste of Rowan, he thought savagely, every muscle in his big body clenching. And she'd give him everything—the slow, consuming build-up, the swift, agonising rapture, and the gentle aftermath, the satisfaction of sated desire...

God, he couldn't even control his thoughts any more, much less use them as he usually did, to distance himself from the importunate demands of his body.

'I dream about you,' she murmured drowsily. 'Wild and free and dominant. Wolfe, take me there...'

The husky, slurred words set him alight. He had to stop this, and stop it now! Mercilessly crushing his hunger, he prevented himself from sliding his hand across the lush, warm curve of her breasts and down, down to the welcoming haven between her legs. 'Do you know exactly what you're asking for?'

Her eyes were gleaming jewels between her long lashes, her mouth a soft, red incitement, the cream silk of her skin flushed. He noticed with a black, hopeless fury the tiny mole on her left shoulder, and more than anything in the world—almost more than he wanted to take her—he wanted to kiss that mark.

The extent of his hunger shocked him, as it had each time they'd made love. Although he wanted her this side of madness, he resented her wild, sweet woman's power over him.

'Mmm,' she whispered. Lifting a boneless hand, she splayed fingers across his heart. With her tongue she followed an invisible line across his throat, murmuring softly, helplessly, as though she found him exquisite to taste.

It was the most primal of claimings. Racked by an aching chill that wiped the sensuality from his body, Wolfe realised that her wandering, ravenous mouth had followed the path an assassin would use to cut his throat.

'Rowan,' he said harshly, pushing her away with hands that shook, fingers that would leave marks on her skin, 'Rowan, damn it, listen to me!'

His angry voice banished that enchanted languor. Shocked, Rowan forced her eyes open. Wolfe's arrogant features were emphasised by an icy intensity in his gaze that stopped her brain from functioning.

She could smell him on her skin, taste him in her mouth, feel his potent masculinity in every nerve. Shame roiled through her in a bitter, painful tide. Oh, God!

What had she been doing? Curling herself around him like a cat on heat?

So appalled she wanted to die, she turned her face away and covered it with her hands.

'It's all right,' he said more gently, but he put her away from him with determination. 'I didn't bring you here to drag you into bed like some sex-starved pirate intent on taking the first woman he's seen in six months.'

Flagrant colour heated her skin as she seized on his statement with an eagerness that owed everything to humiliation. 'So why did you bring me here?' she muttered.

The silk of her camisole abraded the acutely sensitive tips of her breasts. Her body was aflame, greedily desiring satisfaction.

His smile didn't reach the depthless eyes. 'Because I was damned if I was going to talk in front of a room full of people.'

Shivering, Rowan closed her eyes, then forced them open and clenched her teeth as she wooed calm, but all she could bring to mind was the unconstrained strength of the arms that had held her, the heavy, driving beat of Wolfe's heart, and that tantalising, elusive scent. And his warmth, the feeling she'd had of being protected as well as bewitched.

Why had he stopped? Had she disgusted him?

He swore, and then said with raw fury, 'Don't—for God's sake, Rowan, don't. I'm sorry—I thought—Oh, to hell with it! I tried! We can talk later. At the moment I want you past belief, past everything.'

This time he didn't hold back, kissing her with complete abandon, desire stripping away everything but heat and hunger and the fiery pulse of urgency. And Rowan kissed him back without restraint.

This time they made it to the bed. Rowan fought out of her outer layers, but the camisole stayed in place as Wolfe's mouth found the tips of her breasts through the silk, and she tore off his shirt and found his lean hips and pulled him against her so that she could feel his hard desire.

There was very little foreplay—she was ready for him, and slow, skilful seduction didn't get a look-in. They took each other, feasted on each other, lost themselves in sensation and emotion, free at last of the past.

When he entered her she surged up to meet his first hard thrust, striving for that place where sensation ruled supreme. Almost immediately she found it, calling out brokenly as she was flung into an erotic rapture that burnt away everything but her love for him.

He went with her, and then, when she was still gasping into his shoulder, he began to move again.

Heat building inside her into a delirious tumult, she arched her hips into him, answering his silent question with a silent plea. Ruthlessly he used his strength and his considerable expertise to gather her up and push her higher and higher, holding her for an eternity on an exultant, merciless, singing point of existence until the world splintered in unbearable delight and she convulsed again in his arms.

Head thrown back, face carved in agonised pleasure, Wolfe made that primal journey with her, came down with her, and when it was over held her as though she was the most precious thing in his life.

It took long, wonderful minutes before his breathing slowed enough for him to speak. 'Go to sleep now.'

'I thought you wanted to talk,' she said, mumbling the words in a delicious combination of tiredness and laughter.

His chest rose. Drily ironic, he said, 'I've lost the urge. We'll talk in the morning.'

But Rowan woke before then, aching with a sense of loss that bewildered her until she looked across the room and saw him at the window, a big silhouette against the light outside.

She could feel his anger in the quiet room. He was fighting a battle with himself, and she closed her eyes because it seemed obscene to watch him.

But she got out of bed and went across to stand behind him. 'What is it?' she asked gently. 'Your mother?'

Still with his back to her, he said, 'No. I've always thought of myself as a civilised man.'

Rowan's mouth dropped open. Before she could say anything, he went on savagely, 'Do you really want to know why I came to the exhibition?'

She swallowed. 'Why?'

'Because you're mine. My woman. My mate sounds primitive, but I find I am primitive where you're concerned. You belong to me.'

Her heart jumping, she said tentatively, 'So what's wrong with that?'

He turned his head and looked at her. '*You* can ask that? When Tony said exactly the same thing you told him to go to hell.'

Feeling very wise, she said, 'Yes, but I didn't love Tony and he didn't love me. Wolfe, it's as simple as that. Love makes everyone feel primitive—it's quite normal. I feel very primitive and possessive about you—at the exhibition if you hadn't told Tessa Whoever that we were going I'd have seen her off myself.'

He turned and cupped her face, holding it as though she was infinitely precious to him. 'Why are you so certain that I won't behave like Tony?'

'Instinct,' she said with solemn assurance, then smiled radiantly up at him. 'No, more than that. Tony was utterly self-absorbed. You're not. You cared for me when I fell in the water, and even though you threatened me, you listened to me. Tony never did—he only saw and heard what he wanted to see and hear. And you sent Jim to help me fell the oak tree, didn't you?'

'Clever of you to guess,' he said after a startled moment.

Rowan's smile was slow and sweet and mysterious. 'I've learned a bit of how you think. If I hadn't organised this exhibition with as blatant a bit of advertising as you'd find anywhere—I insisted they put that torso with the scar on the brochure—you'd never have come near me, would you?'

'No. Tony's stalking—and the fact that I'd thought it entirely reasonable to harass you about his death—made it impossible. I didn't have the right,' he said distinctly, the deep rasp in his voice very pronounced. 'But I'd have waited the rest of my life for you. Rowan, tell me why you've forgiven me. I didn't expect that.'

She looked into his eyes, seeing into their dark depths for the first time. 'Because I love you, and because I know why you did what you did. I believed that your sleeping with me was just a prelude to extracting information, but I'd lied in a court of law to protect my father. Oh, it was by omission, but I knew Dad had killed Tony. How could I blame you for doing what you could to help your mother?'

He dropped his hands and stepped back, watching her with hooded eyes and a cynical twist to his mouth. 'There's something else, too.'

Her heart compressed in her chest. 'What?'

He said harshly, 'The first time I saw a photograph of

you—the day we met—I recognised the physical power you have over me. But even though I knew that you were the woman who'd been instrumental in Tony's death, I could no more have turned my back on you the night we met than I could have last night.'

'So it wasn't just me,' she said, heart lifting at his frank admission.

'It's never been just you. I went to that first exhibition solely to see you. I didn't plan to meet you, or talk to you.' He smiled mockingly. 'Only my plans exploded in my face the second I set eyes on you. I only have to look at you to want you—hell, I don't even need to see you! Your scent drives me crazy.' He ran a long-fingered hand through his hair and said fiercely, 'And the sound of your voice when you ask if I want milk in my tea makes me want to pick you up and carry you off to bed. It's never happened to me before and it scared me— literally—witless. That first night, and all the time at Kura Bay, I stormed around in a rage of resentment because I was certain you'd made Tony suffer the same bitter hunger, the humiliating loss of autonomy, of independence.'

'I know the feeling,' she said wryly. 'But Tony didn't feel that way, Wolfe. He was utterly sure that he'd make me do what he wanted. That's what scared me so much. I knew that if I gave in it would kill something in me, but towards the end I wondered if eventually I'd get so tired of fighting him that I'd just give in out of exhaustion.'

His hand came out and gripped hers, strength flowing from him to her and back again. 'Not you,' he said grimly. 'For one thing, once we'd met I'd have taken you away from him. But my vast need for you, my inability to control or restrain it, made me angry with both you and myself.'

He raised her hand and kissed it. Rowan shivered as his mouth lingered over the skin.

'You're cold,' he said at once, and moved to close the window.

'I'm not cold,' she told him softly.

In a thickening voice, he murmured, 'Perhaps I need to hold you while I tell you this.'

It would take him time, she realised, before he'd forgotten Tony's legacy enough to feel confident abut her. 'Perhaps,' she agreed, and walked into strong arms that closed around her.

'Anyway,' he said into her hair, 'last night of course I didn't want to talk to you instead of making love, but I felt that I needed to re-establish some sort of control over the situation.'

'Believe me,' she said earnestly, 'it's entirely mutual—I don't make a habit of going to bed with a man I've just met! That first night—when I thought about it afterwards I was awash with shame. I thought I'd gone mad. Do you still resent it?'

'I did until I discovered that you loved me.' He lifted her chin and dropped a kiss onto her expectant mouth, his smile a reckless gleam of white in his dark face. 'It's taken me a long time to admit it, but this is certainly not just a more potent than usual case of lust at first sight. I love you—beyond common sense, beyond idolatry, beyond anything I've ever felt before. I've tried damned hard to kill it, but it won't go.'

Joy exploded within her, joy and an acute, painful relief. Horrified, she felt tears clog her throat. 'And I love you,' she muttered. 'For ever.'

'For ever,' he said deeply, and kissed her brow and

her cheeks, and her mouth, kisses without the violent passion that had linked them from the first, each kiss a promise more binding than marriage vows.

Against his mouth Rowan said quietly, 'Your mother wrote to me a couple of weeks after you left. I was surprised that you told her about Tony.'

He lifted his head and laid his cheek against hers. 'In spite of everything, my mother's a strong woman and she needed to know the truth. She heard me out, and then she said, "I was afraid it was something like that."'

'Had he done it before?'

'Once. I knew nothing about it, and she thought she'd convinced him that it simply wasn't an option. When I told her about you, she grieved because she hadn't got him the help he needed, and she grieved for you, too. And then, being my mother, she did something about it. She's now working in an organisation that helps women who are being stalked.'

'Oh, that's wonderful,' Rowan said, surprised and delighted.

'She's looking forward very much to meeting you,' he told her, a note of concern rasping through his words. 'Although she's scared you might hate her for the rest of your life.'

'Of course I won't,' Rowan said indignantly. 'I never blamed her for Tony's behaviour, and—well, she's your mother. Do you hate my father for—for what he did?'

'No. I understand. I'd kill to protect you too.'

Rowan's heart thudded, then sped up. 'I couldn't tell you,' she said quietly. 'It wasn't just my secret. If you'd been a different man, wanting revenge, my father's superior might have lost everything, and I couldn't do that to him. He'd tried to help in the only way he could— by saying nothing.'

'I know.' He hugged her closely to him, saying into her hair, 'It's over, darling. Let the past go now, and concentrate on the future.'

He loosened one arm, leaning down to switch on a lamp. Every muscle disciplined into passivity, she let him turn her face up again. Greenstone eyes surveyed her with excruciating thoroughness, their golden spangles glittering beneath the thick lashes.

Rowan tried to control the pulses that sped into overdrive as he smiled. Helpless against its hard-edged, masculine magnetism, she drowned in the knowledge of his love.

'Tell me again that you love me,' he commanded.

'I love you.' She said it simply, but with so much conviction that his expression softened.

'Are you going to marry me?'

She hesitated. 'I'm not the sort of wife you need, Wolfe. I'm not the sort of wife any man needs—if you wanted me to give up my work I'd probably do it, but—'

'I'd never ask you to give it up!' he said explosively. 'If you don't want to marry me say so, and we'll organise something else, so long as you understand that you're the only wife I'll ever have,' he finished on a soft growl, his face hard and demanding.

Rowan saw truth in his eyes. Pierced by joy that coloured her skin and warmed her eyes to radiant gold, she said, 'If you can deal with a wife who pots and sculpts, I'll marry you.'

'When? In three days' time?'

Laughing, she said, 'Yes!'

'Well, only on the condition that I never hear you even hint at giving up your work,' he said, touching her trembling mouth with his finger. 'You'll be remembered when I'm long forgotten. Do you want to keep living at Kura Bay?'

'You'll be making enough compromises without having to fly in and out whenever you go away on business trips,' she said, hugging him. 'We can go to Kura Bay for holidays. I'd like to live by the sea, though, if we can do that.'

Laughing deep in his throat, he picked her up. 'Of course we can, although I won't be travelling nearly as much as I have been. We'll buy land by the beach somewhere around Auckland, and build a house with a studio and a state-of-the-art kiln and whatever else you need, suitable—when you're ready—for kids. And we'll be happy, my dearest heart.'

She reached up, kissing his throat. 'Yes,' she said, looking up into his face, her heart in her eyes and her quivering smile. 'Darling Wolfe, I'll marry you and love you and have your children.'

'Then let's do it.' The little galaxies in his eyes danced.

Not fool's gold, she thought as he kissed her with mounting passion and she felt the familiar, ever-precious heat lick through her. No, the true gold of happiness.

Of love.

MAT5

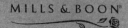

Modern Romance™

THE WEDDING ULTIMATUM by Helen Bianchin

This hugely successful Australian author delivers yet another strong, sexy, sophisticated romance! When Danielle turned to Rafe Valdez to help her family, Rafe promised to make all her problems disappear if she married him and gave him an heir!

HER BABY SECRET by Kim Lawrence

Kim Lawrence delivers a spirited heroine, punchy repartee and sizzling sensuality! Rowena finds flirting with Quinn Taylor exciting, and he clearly wants her — but she's a career woman, with no time for marriage or babies. However, after one passionate night, her feelings change!

SWEET SURRENDER by Catherine George

A strong plot, vivid characterisation and loads of sexual tension, make this a worthy addition to the Dysarts saga! When Alasdair Drummond reappeared in Kate's life she decided she'd lead him to the edge with a teasing affair. Only then the tables were turned on her...

LAZARO'S REVENGE by Jane Porter

The second part of Jane Porter's incredible Galván Brides duet burns with romantic intensity! When Zoe arrives in Argentina, it seems the perfect opportunity for Lazaro to begin his plan of revenge. But the sexual force between them is so strong that Lazaro's plan falls apart...

On sale 3rd May 2002